P

and the

Dogs in Danger

By Helen Haraldsen

Illustrated by Steve Hutton

Petra and the Dogs in Danger

Illustrated by Steve Hutton

Editing, Cover Design and Formatting by Let's Get Booked:
www.letsgetbooked.com

Paperback ISBN: 978-1-913953-07-2

eBook ISBN: 978-1-913953-08-9

Book 2

In memory of Neil Hadfield.

Teacher. Colleague. Friend.

Lover of literature, libraries, language and laughter.

Thank you for believing in me.

ONE

Lucy the Dalmatian and Petra the Pointer closed their eyes against the sun as they licked the ice cream Mrs Daley held for them. It was a warm autumn day, and the dogs had just enjoyed running around on the beach. They were panting and hot, but they couldn't drink the salty sea water, so Mrs Daley had visited the ice cream van. She came back with a vanilla cone for herself and Mr Daley and one for the dogs to share.

"Is that nice, Meist?" Mr Daley asked as Petra licked at her ice cream.

Mr Daley loved coming up with silly names for the dogs. He rarely called them by their real names, preferring to use one of their nicknames. Lucy was often *Lucy Leopard*, or just *Leopard* or *Leps*. She also got *Lu Dog*, *LuLu* and *Lu*. Petra's extra names were even sillier. Mrs Daley had started it by calling her

Flibbertigibbert, as she was such a flighty dog, always disappearing to chase pheasants and rabbits in the woods. This got shortened to *Flib*, *Flibberty*, and *Gibbert*. One day, Mr Daley got the idea to call her *Flibmeister*. Meister means 'master' or 'champion' in German so Mr Daley thought it a great name for her as she was both a German Shorthaired Pointer, and a master of flightiness.

Mr Daley called Petra *Meister* or *Meist* more often than her real name, but she recognised them and knew they were all her names. She wagged her tail to show that she was loving the coolness of the ice cream and was looking forward to crunching through the wafer cone too.

"Oh, look!" They heard an excited voice nearby. "Is that the Dalmatian that lost its spots?" A wide-eyed little boy was pointing at Lucy as he headed towards the beach with his mum.

"Yes, this is Lucy," Mrs Daley answered kindly. This happened to them all the time now. Lucy was a local, if not national, celebrity.

In the spring, Petra had gone missing, and Lucy had been so worried about her, she'd lost all her spots. With a little help from a pug and a wasp, Lucy had been able to find and rescue Petra from a deep hole she'd fallen into. Being reunited with her friend had brought Lucy's spots back, and made her famous. She was 'the Dalmatian that lost its spots' and was now known all over the country. She was even the face of a local pet rescue charity called Peregrine Pets.

"Oh wow! Mum, it's Lucy. She rescued their other dog and got all her spots back!" He was jumping with excitement now.

"I'm so sorry to bother you," the boy's mum said. "But could I take a picture of him with Lucy? He absolutely loves her."

The Daleys obliged, moving themselves and Petra out of the way so the lady could get a picture of her son with Lucy. Lucy turned her head slightly to make sure her best side was towards the camera and smiled. She was an expert canine model and knew how to present herself for the perfect picture.

Petra looked on, her stomach squirming. She loved Lucy. They were best friends. But she couldn't help feeling jealous when she got called 'the other dog' and was pushed out of the picture, unwanted. Until recently, the dogs were always equally admired for their beautiful markings and pretty faces, but since Lucy had become famous for losing her spots, she was the only one people were interested in. Petra was invisible.

Soon, the lady, her son and the ice creams were gone, and it was time to head home in the car. Home for Lucy meant heading straight to her bed for a rest after all the running and playing they'd done on the beach. She needed to recharge. But not Petra. Petra wasn't tired and still wanted to play. As they entered the kitchen, Lucy got into her bed and lay down, but Petra ran straight past. She picked up one of Mr Daley's slippers in her mouth and ran into the living room with it. When Mr Daley realised what she'd done and followed her into the living room, Petra was sitting on the sofa. There was no sign of the slipper.

"What have you done with my slipper, Poltermeist?" Mr Daley asked, using another of his names for Petra. Since Petra had a seemingly magical ability to move things around and make them disappear without being seen, he said she was like a poltergeist: a type of ghost or spirit responsible for objects being moved. And because Petra was a master at making objects in the house – especially shoes, socks and slippers – disappear, she earned another nickname, The Poltermeist.

Later in the evening, after Mr Daley found his missing slipper and everyone had their tea, the family settled themselves on the sofa to watch the evening news. Finally, Petra started to feel sleepy, and she closed her eyes. Snuggling into Mrs Daley, she prepared to enjoy a nap. But just as she was drifting off into a dream involving chasing a rabbit's bobbing white tail, she felt Lucy tense beside her and opened her eyes.

Lucy was sitting bolt upright on the sofa, staring straight at the television. Petra tilted her head so she could see what Lucy was looking at. The screen showed a fawn-coloured pug with a dark face that was vaguely familiar, and a chestnut-coloured Staffordshire Bull Terrier who had a twisted front leg.

"....missing, believed stolen from the garden of Robbins' Veterinary Practice this morning, sometime between ten and half-past..." the newsreader was saying. "Both dogs, named Gomez and Gizmo, belong to vet Wren Robbins." The picture on the screen changed to show the vet smiling with Lucy outside the Peregrine Pets rescue centre, which Lucy had become the face of. Then it showed the vet, live from the waiting room of her surgery. She wasn't smiling now. Her glasses were slightly clouded, but the red rims of her eyes and glossy cheeks showed that she'd been crying.

"If anyone sees them or knows where they are," she said into the microphone, her voice shaking, "please bring them back. They're my family. I...can't bear not knowing where they are or what's happened to them. I can't concentrate. I need them here, where they're safe. I can give a reward. Just please, get in touch if you see them. Please..."

"Oh no, poor Wren. What an awful thing to happen," said Mr Daley.

"I know. It's terrible. I'd heard there'd been a spate of dog thefts in the area recently. We'll have to be extra careful with these two." Mrs Daley put a protective arm around Lucy.

"Look at LuLu," Mr Daley said, watching Lucy staring at the TV. "It's like she recognises them and understands what's happened."

"Don't be silly dear, she's just looking because she knows they're dogs."

But Mrs Daley was wrong. Lucy understood every word.

"Petra," she whined. "Petra, wake up. Gomez and Gizmo have been stolen! Gomez helped me rescue you. I couldn't have done it without him. We have to help. We have to find them and get them home."

TWO

When Mr and Mrs Daley went to bed, and the dogs were alone in the kitchen, Lucy continued to talk about rescuing Gomez and Gizmo.

"But of course we don't know where they are," she said. "If only I could find the wasp who helped me find you. He'd be able to guide us to them."

"Does it have to be that particular wasp? Couldn't you ask any wasp?" Petra said.

"Other wasps can't communicate with us," Lucy explained. "They talk to each other without words, but this wasp is special. He's taught himself to speak human and some of the animal languages as well. We can't do this without him. Tomorrow I'll have to go in the garden and see if I can call to him."

Eventually, Lucy dropped off to sleep. Petra remained awake, thinking. If there was to be a rescue, it should be her that did it. Alone. She was fast, and her colouring meant she was always well camouflaged. She was The Poltermeist – the master at moving things without being seen. This was the job for her. If Petra could rescue Gomez and Gizmo, she'd be a hero. Like Lucy, people would recognise her. They'd want to have their pictures taken with her. She could be on the news and become known as the pointer who rescued stolen dogs. If Lucy came along, she'd slow her down. Lucy couldn't jump fences like she could. She couldn't run up and down steep slopes and through undergrowth effortlessly like Petra. Lucy was much slower, and with her bright white coat and black spots, Lucy was never camouflaged. She was always visible. Even worse, now she was famous, she'd be spotted immediately. They'd be picked up and returned home before they even got out of their own village if Lucy came. It had to be Petra on her own, but how could she convince Lucy to stay at home and let her go by herself?

Petra's dreams that night were filled with rehearsals of conversations with Lucy, rather than the usual dreams of chasing the bobbing white tails of rabbits and deer.

In the morning, Lucy dashed straight out to the garden to see if there were any wasps on the fuchsia. She was in luck; a number of bees and wasps dangled from the brightly coloured flowers.

"Hello, sorry, excuse me," Lucy began. "I'm looking for a wasp. He's a very special wasp; he can speak several languages. Do you know him? Could you get a message to him for me? Some dogs have been stolen, and I need his help to find them...if possible." Lucy looked at the wasps, hoping that one might wiggle an antenna to show it had heard her. But they carried on flitting from flower to flower, showing no sign at all that they'd seen or heard the Dalmatian who was talking to them.

Lucy's tail drooped. "It's no good. These wasps don't understand a word I'm saying. We're going to need another way to find where Gomez and Gizmo have been taken."

As it was a warm, sunny day and Mrs Daley had the day off work, the dogs were able to stay outside in the garden sunbathing. Or at least, that's what Mrs Daley thought they were doing as they lay in the grass.

Actually, they were thinking. Lucy was straining her brain for a new plan. Petra was daydreaming about returning from a daring rescue mission with the missing dogs at her side.

Unable to come up with an alternative plan, Lucy got up to get a drink. Just as she'd finished lapping water from the bowl, a wasp alighted on the rim.

"Greetingzzz! I've heard you've been asking for me, my lady? You need my assistanzzz?"

"Oh, wasp! You came. It's so good to see you again. I never got to thank you for helping me to rescue Petra."

"No thankzzz needed. It was my pleasure to help you. Now you need my help again?"

"How did you know? The wasps I asked this morning just ignored me. I didn't think they'd understood a word I'd said."

"They didn't, but when they came back to the nest and started communicating in our language about a strange spotty dog who seemed to be trying to speak to them, I knew it could only be you. I asked them where you were and came straight here. I am at your service."

Lucy wagged her tail as she relayed the story of the missing dogs to the wasp. "You found Petra when she was missing, even though she was at the bottom of a deep hole. I hoped that you, and maybe your friends, might be able to do it again and find Gomez and Gizmo so we can go and get them and bring them home?"

"Ahh, Gomez, the unhelpful pug. Yes, I remember him. It's like I told him: you should alwayzzz help when you can as you never know when you might need help yourself."

"He learned his lesson, I think. I couldn't have got Petra home without him. He deserves to come home too, and Gizmo. Will you help?"

"Of course! I'll go now and spread the word. We'll have the stolen dogs found in no time."

And with that, he buzzed off.

THREE

The Daleys wondered if Lucy was all right as she was so restless and wouldn't stop pacing around the house. By the time she'd spoken to the wasp in the garden, there hadn't been many hours of daylight left for his search to begin. Petra didn't understand why the wasps couldn't search during the night. Couldn't they use their noses, like dogs, to find their way? Lucy had to explain that she didn't know about a wasp's sense of smell, but she could remember being told that they can't navigate without the sun and can't fly once it gets cold at night.

The next day was nice once again, and the dogs were able to spend it in the garden while the Daleys did some gardening. Hours passed with no sign of the wasp. Lucy was worried they'd be taken back inside before he brought news. Or maybe he didn't have any. Maybe they hadn't been able to find Gomez and Gizmo.

Her stomach fluttered as she wondered why they'd been taken, where they could be and what might be happening to them. She hoped they were still together at least.

The Daleys worked hard all day, cutting the grass, trimming back trees and bushes and digging weeds from the flower beds. Petra tried to help by digging a hole in the garden, but this made Mrs Daley very cross. Apparently, digging up the grass was very bad indeed, and poor Petra got told off. "If only you could be trained to dig up the weeds instead of wrecking the lawn," Mrs Daley said, filling in the hole Petra had dug.

By the time they were finished, the Daleys were weary and hungry. The evening was still warm so they decided to eat their tea outside to admire the results of their efforts. It was while they were all outside, the Daleys eating, the dogs begging for treats, that they heard a buzzing that sounded more urgent than the gentle drone of the bees and wasps sleepily dipping in and out of the flowers.

Lucy tore her eyes away from the forkful of food heading towards Mr Daley's mouth and looked around her for the wasp. She saw that he had landed near them on a pink rose.

"Wasp! Any news? Have you found them?"

"Yezzz, we have found your friendzzz," he answered.

"Oh! That's such good news," Lucy felt like her spots were dancing with excitement all over her body. "Where are they? Can you lead us to them?"

"It'zzz not so simple, I'm afraid," said the wasp. "The dogs are many miles away in the south of the county. If you travel as the wasp flies, instead of following the roads the humans use, it isn't as far, but the route will be difficult for you. There are rivers, lakes, hedges and mountains in the way. And, the place where Gomezzz and Gizmo are being held is well guarded by the biggest dogzzz I've ever seen. There are lots of dogzzz inside. It'zzz some kind of doggy prison. I can't see how you can get inside in the first place, never mind get your friendzzz out of there."

"We can't just rescue Gomez and Gizmo if there are other dogs trapped in there. We have to get them all out. What do the thieves want so many dogs for? How many others are there?" Lucy said.

"I don't know, I'm afraid. It'zzz too dark inside the building they're being kept in for uzzz to see them."

"Well, if you can't see them, how do you know there are others besides Gomez and Gizmo?" Petra asked.

"We can smell them. It stinkzzz in there. It wazzz so bad we almost suffocated. We couldn't see, and we couldn't breathe. We had to get out quickly," the wasp replied.

"This is terrible." Lucy's spots stopped dancing, and she sat down, frowning. "We've got to get them out of there, but how?"

Petra knew this was the time for her to put forward her plan of going alone. But she needed to do it carefully. She didn't want to offend Lucy or let it be known that she was keen to lead the rescue by herself so that she could claim the glory.

"Erm...I think that it would be better for me to go to them. Just me," she started.

"Just you?" Lucy gasped. "On your own? No, it's too risky. What if something happened to you? No-one would know where you were. I can't go through that again, the worrying. We need to do it together. It's too big a job for one dog on its own." Lucy's frown deepened, the white ridges on her face looking like snow-covered mountains.

Petra took a deep breath and explained how Lucy would endanger the mission. She was too easy to see at the best of times, but now that she was famous, she wouldn't be able to go anywhere without being noticed immediately. "Unless we can travel at night, you'd be spotted within minutes, and we'd be brought home. We'd get nowhere," she pointed out gently.

"We can't travel at night. We'd need the wasp to guide us and he can't fly in the dark," Lucy whined.

"I could go first thing in the morning," Petra said. "You know that I can run and jump and swim all day. Plus, I'm good at being invisible, like a ghost. I can get there faster on my own. We don't know what the thieves plan to do with Gomez and Gizmo so I need to get them out as soon as possible."

Lucy frowned. She knew that Petra was right. It would be awful for her to be left behind, worrying about Petra and the other dogs, but she hadn't to be selfish. She had to do what was best. Lucy would stay behind and look after the Daleys. Reluctantly, she accepted a piece of chicken Mr Daley was offering her. She'd lost her appetite but didn't want to be rude.

"All right," she said. "You can set off at first light in the morning. Tonight, when the Daleys go to bed, we'll have to see if we can work out how to turn keys and open doors. You'll need to be able to let yourself out before they get up, and you might have to open locked doors where you're going too. Wasp, can you be here as soon as it's light in the morning?"

"Of courzzz," he said, bowing over the edge of the rose he was sitting on. "I'll be here."

The Daleys had finished their meal and were getting ready to carry the plates back inside. "Come on, girls," Mrs Daley said. "Let's go in."

"Come on then," Lucy said to Petra. "We've got work to do."

FOUR

True to his word, the wasp was at the kitchen window at first light the next morning. Lucy and Petra could see him walking in impatient circles around the window pane, no doubt wondering why Petra wasn't outside waiting to set off, as they'd agreed.

During the night, Lucy quietly showed Petra how to jump up and use her paw to press down the door handle and open it into the living room. Then she'd pushed it, so it was almost closed again, and demonstrated how to use nose and claws to pull it back open towards her. Petra had quickly learned how to do this, so they'd turned their attention to the front door that led outside. Pressing down the handle was no problem, but the door was locked. Lucy had watched the Daleys turn the key many times and understood that turning it towards the coat pegs unlocked it, and turning it towards the living room door locked it. The two dogs tried for hours to use their paws and teeth to turn the key and unlock the door, but they couldn't manage it. Eventually, Lucy decided they would have to leave it as Petra needed a good night's sleep before her journey in the morning.

When the dark kitchen lightened as the sun rose, and the wasp arrived, the Daleys weren't up yet. Lucy tried again to grapple with the key, but it was small and stiff, and she couldn't get it to turn. She whined and cried in frustration.

At last, they heard Mrs Daley's footsteps coming down the stairs. Despite being in a desperate hurry to get going, Lucy saw an opportunity to make the most of the delay. She and Petra had to pretend to be calm. If they were up and bouncing with excitement, Mrs Daley would think they were desperate for the toilet and would let them out immediately. Although that was what they wanted, Lucy knew that to do so would be sending Petra out on an empty stomach. She might as well have some breakfast before she left.

Lucy climbed back into bed and told Petra to do the same. Then she pretended to be asleep. "Wait," she breathed quietly at Petra, knowing how impatient her friend was.

"Look at you two sleepy puppies. I thought you were crying to go out." Mrs Daley greeted them as she entered the kitchen and bent down to give them both a pat. She put the kettle on then put the dogs' breakfast dishes down for them.

"Now," Lucy said. Petra understood and leapt from her bed to gobble first her own bowl of biscuits, then Lucy's too, while Mrs Daley had her back turned to pour hot water into a mug. When she turned around, Lucy was standing by her dish, wagging her tail.

"You two are hungry this morning," Mrs Daley said, having no idea that Petra had eaten both breakfasts. "Time to go out for a wee-wee now."

With that, she walked back through the house and opened the back door to allow the dogs into the garden for five minutes while she drank her tea.

"At last!" buzzed the wasp. "I wondered if you'd changed your mind."

"Sorry, we couldn't get out. Turns out, mastering keys is harder than I thought," Lucy explained before turning to Petra. "Please be careful," she implored, rubbing her nose against her friend's. "Whatever happens, stay safe and look after yourself. I want you back here as soon as possible. Our poor humans will be frantic with worry that you've gone... again."

"Let's hope you don't lose your spots again," Petra joked, excited about the adventure that lay ahead of her. "Don't worry about me. I won't fall into any holes this time!"

"You'd better not. I know you'll be moving fast, but just remember to look where you're going and listen to the wasp. There may be danger on the way, not to mention the thieves when you get there. Watch you don't end up getting dognapped yourself."

"Yes, ma'am!"

"Oh, I wish I was coming with you," Lucy said.

"Yes, but, as we've said, it's best that I go on my own. You still have an important job to do here – looking after the humans."

Lucy sighed. "Well, you'd better get going before she comes back to take us for a walk. Good luck."

With that, Petra turned and, quick as a flash, climbed up and over the gate at the bottom of the garden and dashed away across the fields that lay beyond it.

"Hey, wait for me!" the wasp exclaimed. "You don't even know where you're going. I'm supposed to be the guide!"

Without a further word to Lucy, he whizzed off in pursuit of the crazy pointer who was galloping off into the distance with no clue where she needed to go.

Typical Petra, thought Lucy as she heard Mrs Daley entering the garden through the front gate, ready to take the dogs for their morning walk. She was calling their names. *Here we go again.*

Lucy trotted up to Mrs Daley, who put her on the lead, still calling Petra's name.

"Where's that naughty dog?" Mrs Daley said, her lips pursed in annoyance at Petra's latest disappearing act. She always seemed to be vanishing into thin air, and the Daleys often played a game of 'spot the pointer' on walks when Petra melted into the scenery, camouflaged by her markings. Her expression changed as an awful thought occurred to her. "What if she's been stolen like the vet's dogs? Has someone taken her Lu? Why would they take Petra and leave you behind?"

Lucy rubbed her head against Mrs Daley's legs, trying to show her that there was nothing to worry about, but Mrs Daley didn't understand.

"I'm calling the police," she said, hurrying back into the house, the morning walk forgotten about.

The police won't find Petra, Lucy thought. *No-one will. She's The Poltermeist;* a phantom dog. Not only does she make *things* go missing, she's good at going missing herself!

FIVE

Petra travelled like the wind. Even the wasp struggled to keep up with her and had to hitch a ride on her collar to give his wings a rest. He'd never met a creature with as much stamina. Petra raced through fields and leapt over fences like an Olympic hurdler. She squeezed through hedges, hurtled over fells and mountains and crossed rivers and lakes. A swim across one of them went unnoticed by the people sailing along on the lake cruiser, and soon, Petra was climbing out on the other side. She gave herself a big shake to get rid of all the water dripping from her coat.

"Oi!" said the wasp indignantly as a large water drop bashed into him and knocked him to the ground. "Can you give me some warning next time you do that? You nearly drowned me."

"Sorry," said Petra. Her heart was pounding from all the running, jumping and swimming, but she was keen to press on. "Where now?"

"Don't you need a rest? Some food?" the wasp asked.

"No, I'm fine. Let's keep moving."

"You might not need fuel, but I do. I can smell food. Come on, over here."

The wasp flew a little way up the grass bank beside the lake, where a picnic had been left uncovered. Drawn by the sugary smell of fizzy pop, the wasp was distracted by a plate of fruit and landed on a raspberry.

"Mmmm, so tasty," he cried. "Come on, Petra. Eat something."

Petra hadn't felt hungry until she saw the food. She managed to gobble a pork pie, a block of cheese, several sandwiches and a sponge cake filled with delicious jam and cream before she heard shrieks coming from the water and noticed a group of people running towards her. They looked angry.

Annoyed that she'd drawn attention to herself, Petra hurriedly slunk away into the shadow of the trees. *So much for staying invisible,* she thought.

Feeling recharged from her brief rest and stolen lunch, Petra was ready to run again. Mile after mile, she covered effortlessly. Petra enjoyed running free without having to worry about anyone else. There was no-one calling her name, pulling her away from her adventures. It was pure, exhilarating freedom. Her heart almost burst with the thrill of it.

"Slow down, the place is just over this hill," the wasp told her, interrupting her celebrations and reminding her that she had a job to do, "and keep low. You don't want to be seen."

Petra's heart felt like a balloon that had been popped as she crept over the hill and saw the place the wasp said was 'it'. She'd just been enjoying the feel of her blood racing through her veins, the wind in her face, the smells coming to her from the land and air, the grass, moss and soil under her paws, being free, untamed and wild. But that ended like a slammed door when she saw it. Petra froze and lifted a front paw. Like a statue, she observed the target.

It was a compound surrounded by a high metal fence, lined with metal sheets to screen what was inside. There was a rough, pot-holed track to reach the padlocked gates at the front, but otherwise, it was in the middle of nowhere, surrounded by fields and bordered by woodland. From her position looking down from the hillside, Petra could see that a number of buildings lay within the compound, but they weren't houses. Most of them were made out of metal and looked like shipping containers. Some looked like plastic and had windows, but the curtains were drawn. That would be where the humans would be, Petra guessed. Patrolling the area between the locked gates and the building were two enormous mastiffs. They were the biggest dogs Petra had ever seen. One was brown and could easily be mistaken for a grizzly bear, while the other was a lighter colour and resembled a lion with its thick, shaggy mane of hair. Both dogs were fastened by their collars to chains, which dragged and clanked across the ground as they paced around. They were guards, and they were guarding a prison.

"I've got to get in there?" Petra whispered to the wasp. "How can I get in there, past those two? There's no way in."

"I did tell you that," the wasp pointed out. "Perhapzzz it would've been a good idea to have a plan before you set off?"

Petra didn't answer. She knew he was right but didn't want to admit it. She'd been too hasty just thinking of the end result: the glory she'd receive for rescuing Gomez and Gizmo and reuniting them with their owner. She hadn't given a thought to *how* she was going to get them out. Or even how she was going to get in to find them. She gulped, wishing Lucy was there with her. Lucy was the one who was good at thinking things through. She'd know what to do.

A pang of guilt prodded at Petra. She hadn't given Lucy a single thought since she'd left her behind in the garden that morning. Petra hadn't missed her. She did now. She wished she hadn't persuaded Lucy to stay at home because she would have slowed them down. In her impatience to get started on the rescue mission, Petra hadn't even considered what she would do when she got there. Thinking back, the wasp had told them it was a prison and that it was guarded by huge dogs, but she hadn't taken it in. She'd been in too much of a rush. All she'd thought about was getting here. But now what?

The realisation that it was up to her sank in like a stone making its way to the bottom of a deep lake. There was no-one else to rely on. The air was turning chilly, and the sun was low in the sky to the west. It would be dark soon. And cold. There'd be no snuggling on the sofa with the Daleys tonight. No nice warm bed in the kitchen with Lucy.

Petra shivered.

"What do you think?" she asked the wasp, hoping that he might be able to offer some advice. There was no answer. "Wasp? Wasp? Where are you?"

Petra turned about, desperately seeking out her companion. He was gone. Just as Lucy had experienced, once the wasps showed the target's location, their job was over. He'd gone to find shelter somewhere for the night. She was alone.

What do I do now? Petra wondered as the sun sank lower behind the trees.

SIX

Petra watched and waited until the sky turned dark. A light came on in one of the plastic buildings, and the men she'd seen moving around disappeared inside it. They didn't come back out again. Still, Petra waited.

The two enormous guard dogs lay around for a while, close to the gates, but eventually they took themselves off into their kennels, clanking their chains as they went.

Petra was cold and her stomach rumbled, but she forced herself to wait. When it got dark at home, Mr and Mrs Daley sat on the sofa and watched the TV for a while, but eventually they switched off all the lights and went to bed. They didn't reappear until the next morning. Petra was counting on these humans doing the same. That was the time to try and sneak in: while the humans and guard dogs slept. She'd find Gomez and Gizmo, get them out, and they could travel home through the night. She'd be able to find her way back by following her own scent trail, and if they kept moving all night, they could be back home in the morning before the thieves awoke and realised the two dogs were missing.

Petra kept waiting. At last, the lights in the plastic building went out. The night was silent, but the almost full moon meant that she could still see well enough as she crept down the slope towards the compound.

There was no way in. Every inch of the fence was lined with metal sheets that went right into the ground. She couldn't squeeze under it. There were no gaps to get through; it was too high to jump and too smooth to climb. Petra went right round the perimeter of the compound twice, hoping she'd find something she'd missed. She didn't. Petra couldn't believe it. It was the first time she'd ever found a place she couldn't get into by going over, under or through.

Petra wanted to howl in desperation, but she couldn't; it would wake everyone up. She had to keep quiet and find a way in. She just had to. This was nothing like she'd imagined. In her daydream, she'd bravely travelled across the land to where the stolen dogs were being held, got them out, returned them home and received a hero's welcome. Yet here she was, stuck at the first obstacle. Never mind getting the dogs out; she couldn't even get in. Petra had failed. Already.

Sitting down under a tree, Petra looked up at the moon and thought of Lucy. She wondered if she was asleep, all cosy in her bed. Or maybe she was awake, worrying about her. Suddenly, Petra got a sense of what it must have been like for Lucy when she was out, all alone in the dark looking for her missing friend. It wasn't quite the exciting adventure Petra had imagined. It was difficult, frustrating and dispiriting. And she hadn't even got started yet.

But, she told herself, you got here. You achieved the first part of the mission. Now it's part two. Take it step by step. Gomez and Gizmo are in there somewhere, and you're going to get them out. You can't give up. Think. There has to be a way to get in.

While Petra sat thinking, she became aware of a sound. It was a tiny sound, like a drop of water plopping into a puddle. Petra's ears pricked towards the noise. She got up and moved towards it, not sure what she was going to find.

A glint caught her eye. It was a reflection of the moon on water. In the corner of the compound there was what looked like a stream flowing under the metal fence. Except it wasn't a stream. It was a very short, narrow channel; just a ditch really. The water in it didn't flow like a stream; it was still and unmoving. As

Petra got closer, she wrinkled her nose. An unpleasant smell wafted from the water. She wondered how she'd missed it on her previous inspections – probably because she was in too much of a hurry – but she gave a hopeful little wag of her tail. *Could this be a way in?*

The watery ditch did pass under the fence and into the compound, but a metal grille fastened to the bottom of the fence prevented entry. The only option would be to go under the water to pass beneath the metal grille.

Petra wrinkled her nose more. *Can I do it?* She was very happy to swim in lakes and rivers... even the sea, but this water was dirty and smelly, and she'd have to put her whole body and face under the water to get past the grille. Everything in her told her not to do it. But she knew she had to. There was no other way. Her heart raced as she took a deep breath and slipped silently into the dark water.

It wasn't as cold as she'd expected, but it felt thick and smothering, like it wanted to drown her. Petra closed her eyes and held her breath to pass under the grille. As the water closed over her head, Petra felt like she was being swallowed. It only took seconds to pass under the grille, but it felt like a lifetime. Petra broke from the water and scrambled out on the other side as if a crocodile was snapping at her tail.

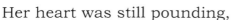

Her heart was still pounding,

and her whole body

felt slimy, but

she'd done it.

She was in.

SEVEN

Lucy's 'how-to-open-a door-handle' lessons paid off, and Petra was glad that, for once, she'd taken the time to practise something. The metal building she'd seen the humans going in and out of as she watched from the hillside had a door with a handle like the one at home. Petra jumped up against it and pressed her paw down on the handle like Lucy had shown her, using her weight to push the door. For a second, nothing happened, and Petra worried that it was locked. But soon, she felt the door swing away. Fortunately for her, the humans thought that the metal fence, padlocked gates and fierce guard dogs were enough to keep intruders out. But they hadn't kept Petra out, and as she stepped eagerly inside the building, she found what they were so desperate to hide from prying eyes.

The room was as dark as an underground cave. There were no windows to let any moonlight in, so Petra had to rely on her other senses. Like the wasp had said, it absolutely stank inside, and Petra wished she could close her nostrils as the smells swooped around her. She staggered as she took in what they were telling her.

Dogs. Not one or two. Many. She could smell their poo and wee... and fear. She recognised the scent from her time 'rabbit ratching' as Mr Daley called it, when Petra disappeared into the brambles, searching for rabbits.

Rabbits were exciting to hunt. Petra knew they often sheltered in the brambles, and it was electrifying to find one as they suddenly dashed away, white tails bobbing like an invitation to be chased. The scent of fear that came from them, as they ran away from her, was exactly the same as the smell in this room. Only now, it had the opposite effect. In here, it made Petra want to run away instead of move towards it. Hackles rose from the base of her neck, along her back, all the way to the top of her tail. *Run,* her brain screamed at her. *You're in danger; get out!*

And she nearly did. Any confidence she might have had about her quest disappeared like the wasp. She'd turned around and was ready to flee back out of the door and run all night to get back home until another smell reached her. A smell that stopped her in her tracks. Petra recognised it but hadn't known she remembered it until now. She could just make it out, buried under the layers of everything else. It was the smell of puppies.

A memory leapt into her mind of herself with her brothers and sisters suckling from their mother. The memory moved on to one of them all climbing on top of each other and playing together in their puppy pen.

Then she remembered the room it had been in: a kitchen. A lovely light room with a big window and a door that was often open into the garden so that, when they were old enough, the puppies could go outside and explore. There had been a cage in the corner of the room in which sat a large, red bird with multi-coloured wings and a white beak. She'd never thought of that bird since she'd come to live with the Daleys and Lucy, but now she remembered how that bird used to mimic the woman in the house. The bird would yell, 'Boston, get in your bed…now!" and Petra's father, who was called Boston, wouldn't know it was the bird and would get in his bed, thinking the woman had told him.

Happy times. Petra's puppyhood had been filled with light, warmth and fun. But there were puppies in here. In the dark, in the dirt. She couldn't see them, but she felt their presence. She knew that they, and their mothers, were afraid.

The wasp *had* said there were many dogs in the prison, but Petra had pushed it to the back of her mind as she hadn't wanted to think about it. Her self-appointed mission was to rescue Gomez and Gizmo. She thought the wasp was probably exaggerating, and she could never have imagined this horror as being reality.

Petra turned away from the open door that was inviting her back to her freedom and resisted the impulse to leave this place behind. "Hello?" she called very softly in case she woke the sleeping guard dogs outside. They'd been snoring as she crept past them, rumbling like trains, but a loud noise could easily wake them. "Gomez? Gizmo? Are you in here?"

"Who's that?" she heard a trembling voice ask.

"Nobody. Just go back to sleep," came the reply.

Petra inched forward. She'd never moved so slowly in her life. It was as if the sense of dread in the room had attached lead weights to her. She could barely move. "Gomez, Gizmo… are you here?" she tried again.

"There *is* someone here! It's a dog! It's come from outside!"

Rustling noises made Petra's ears prick, and she could just about detect some shapes in the gloom from the tiny amount of light coming in through the door she'd left open. She could now make out that the inside of the building was split into pens: a row on the left and a row on the right with a corridor between them. The pens had tall walls around them, and the entrance to each one had a man-height door covered in mesh. Standing at the door of each pen was a dog.

"Who is it?" a small voice asked again.

"I don't know," came the reply.

"Have they come to let us out of here?" the voice asked.

There was no answer, but Petra detected a change to the air in the room. It was moving. Dogs were wagging their tails. None of them spoke or asked if it was true: was she there to get them out? But their wagging tails told her that they were hoping. They were looking to her to get them out of this dark, stinking prison. But could she do it? Petra gulped.

I only came here to rescue two dogs, she said to herself, *not a kennel full. Not puppies! What am I going to do?*

How she wished she had Lucy with her.

EIGHT

"Here to help us...."

"...let us out."

"Get back home."

The dogs' whispers reached out to Petra, pulling her towards them. There was a husky on the right and a cocker spaniel on the left in the first pens she reached. The light was limited, but Petra could tell that the husky was strong, fit and healthy. The spaniel, on the other hand, was not. Even in the darkness, Petra could tell that her coat was matted and she was thin. Lying in some dirty straw behind her lay three newborn puppies.

In the pen next to her was a border terrier. She had visible bald patches in her coat and a runny nose. A litter of puppies huddled behind her too. Opposite her was a brown and white border collie. The collie was

62

pacing around her pen, desperate to get out. Just like the husky, she looked fit and healthy.

Petra continued up the central aisle. The other dogs in the pens on the right side were in good condition: a greyhound, a dachshund and in the final pen, Petra was shocked to find a young Dalmatian. Not a puppy, but not fully grown either; Petra guessed she must be around four to five months old.

On the other side, it was a different story. As well as the spaniel and terrier, there was a poodle who also had a litter of pups, and a boxer, who, despite being heavily in pup had bones and ribs protruding from every part of her body. In the last pen on the left were two small dogs. They weren't pups, though. One was a pug. The other was a Staffordshire Bull Terrier.

"Gomez?" Petra's eyes widened. "Gizmo?" Was it them? Had she found them?

"Who are you?" Gomez asked.

"I'm Petra," she said. "You helped Lucy, the Dalmatian that lost its spots to find me earlier this year when I went missing. I'm here to repay the favour."

"You're Petra?" Gomez sounded like he couldn't believe it. "And you've come to get us out of here? It's true…" he sounded like he was talking to himself now. "The wasp said that you should always help others when you can, as you never know when you'll be the one who needs help.

"Oh, thank you for finding us. Gizmo, Petra here is going to get us out and take us home." He nudged his friend, who was lying on the cold metal floor.

"Well, I had some help in finding you," Petra said, "And I'm afraid I need some more if I'm going to get you out. I've learned how to open doors with handles, but I don't know how to open these."

The pen doors didn't have handles that she could open. They had bolts that needed to be pushed up and slid back. Petra had no idea how to deal with them.

"Ah ha!" said Gomez, suddenly wiggling his bottom. "I know! They're the same as the ones at the vets. I had to get one open to let Lucy out so she could come and find you. I had to use a goose feather to reach, but you're tall. You don't need a feather."

Gomez patiently explained the steps Petra needed to take to open the door.

Petra stood up on her hind legs so that her head was level with the metal barrel bolt. Following Gomez's instructions, Petra used her snout to nose up the latch so that it was sticking out towards her. Next, she needed to take the latch in her teeth and pull it back. But it was difficult. The latch was only small, and Petra couldn't get a good grip on it. Her teeth kept slipping off the cold metal, and her back legs began to shake. She dropped onto all fours to take a rest.

Gomez understood exactly how she felt. He remembered how his mouth had ached, and his legs had trembled when he'd struggled to release Lucy from her pen at the vets. He recalled how he'd wanted to give up, but Lucy and the wasp had encouraged him until he finally succeeded in opening the door. He remembered too how wonderful it had felt when his hard work paid off. The reflection on that day also brought to mind how he'd refused to help at first, and had to be threatened with a wasp sting to get out of bed. Gomez shook his head to try and dislodge that memory. He was ashamed of it. But he'd learned a lesson from it and now tried to look out for those in need. Twice he'd taken his vet owner into the garden to show her where injured birds were hiding so that she could help them. And now he could help Petra.

"I know it's hard," he said to her through the wire mesh of the door. "Have a rest, but don't give up. You can do it."

Petra was a determined dog and had no intention of giving up. She was soon taking the bolt in her teeth again. Instead of trying to give one, big pull, Petra worked on moving the bolt millimetre by millimetre. She'd never had to be so patient in her life. Normally, she did everything in a big rush. She was no good at waiting. But the bolt wouldn't be rushed, so she had to take her time. Eventually, she felt the bolt release from the keeper on the door frame. She'd done it! She'd unlocked the door! It didn't swing open, though. It needed to be opened towards her.

"I need you two to push it from your side," she instructed Gomez and Gizmo. The two dogs used their heads to push against the door until it opened a little. Then Petra hooked her paw around it, as Lucy had shown her, and pulled it open. In no time, Gomez and Gizmo were standing beside her in the corridor between the pens.

I've done it; I've freed them. Now all I need to do is get them out of here and go home, Petra thought. "Come on then," she said, feeling as light as air. "Let's get out of here."

"Wait!" the border collie spoke. "Get me out too. I have to get home to my farm. I'm needed. I've got work to do."

"Me too," said the husky. "I want to go home. Let me out and take me with you."

Soon the Dalmatian, the greyhound and the dachshund were joining in too. Petra hesitated. The other dogs weren't her responsibility. It would be harder work to get seven dogs back home rather than just two. She knew who Gomez and Gizmo belonged to, but what about the others? Where were their homes? Did they expect her to know? It was too much. She needed to get out, back into the fresh air. She moved towards the door that would take her outside.

"Please don't leave us in here," the collie pleaded as Petra passed her pen.

"We can't leave them," Gomez said, trotting up behind Petra. "We have to get them out too."

Petra's heart sank. This wasn't what she'd planned, but as she contemplated leaving the other dogs in their dark, dirty pens, she knew she couldn't. Gomez was right.

As she got to work on opening the collie's door, it occurred to Petra that these dogs must also have been stolen, just like Gomez and Gizmo. *If I can get them all back to their owners,* she thought, *it'll make me even more of a hero. I could end up being more famous than Lucy.* She closed her eyes, ignoring her aching teeth, and pulled hard on the bolt.

NINE

Soon, eight dogs stood in the corridor between the pens. Once the collie was released, she'd joined in with helping Petra to open the other doors. Petra was rather put out that the collie could pull the bolts back faster than her, but grateful that she hadn't had to do them all herself. Her hind legs felt like jelly and her teeth hurt.

"Right, let's go," Petra said, her impatience to get out returning.

"But what about the others?" said Gizmo, looking at the pens on the left. The dogs on that side had remained silent as the others had been released. Not a whimper came from them and, unlike the others, none of them had begged to be released. The three dogs with puppies had gone back to them. Only the boxer remained, gazing through the mesh. Her muzzle drooped, and wrinkles creased her face into a picture of despair.

"Go." It was barely a whisper. "Get out of here while you can. We can't come with you. The others have new puppies, and I'm due to have mine any day. They'll be blind, deaf and completely helpless. We can't leave them," her voice cracked. "Go on, now before they catch you."

Something about the boxer made Petra stop. Just moments ago, she'd been desperate to escape this prison, but the dog's sadness pulled her back.

"I'm sorry," she said through the mesh. "If I can, I'll come back for you. When your pups are a bit bigger, I'll come and get you out. All of you." Petra blinked in surprise at herself. She'd had no idea she was going to say that or where it had come from.

"Thank you," the boxer gave a feeble wag of her tail. "You're a kind soul to come here and rescue all of these dogs. Good luck in getting home safely, but watch your backs. The men who brought them here will be angry they've gone. They'll look for them and bring them back if they catch them. And you too."

Petra's hackles rose at the thought of the thieves tracking them, hunting them down to catch them and return them to the cages. She herself could end up being captured if she wasn't careful. There'd be no glory then. She'd spend the rest of her life trapped in the darkness and her family would have no idea where she was. Petra had been bred to hunt, to find prey and flush it out. Mr and Mrs Daley didn't hunt and hadn't trained Petra to either, but it was in her. Instinctively, she was always searching for wild animals to chase but she'd never dreamed that she would become the prey. That she'd be the one being hunted. And it wasn't just her; there were eight of them. How were eight dogs going to avoid being seen as they travelled back home?

Petra's heart trembled. She hadn't thought this through. She'd imagined travelling through the night and being back home by morning. But now, she knew that wasn't going to happen. On her own, she could move unseen with the speed and stealth of a ghost. As part of a pack, that would be impossible.

Unlike Lucy, who often stopped for a sniff and a wag, and sometimes a play with other dogs they met on walks, Petra had no interest in other dogs. She was always too busy to be sociable. Now here she was lumbered with this mis-matched crew who were all looking to her to get them out of here. If it was just the Dalmatian, husky, collie, and the greyhound, it wouldn't be so bad. They were all big, athletic dogs who could move fast. The pug, staffy and dachshund were a different matter, though, with their short legs, not to mention Gizmo's twisted front leg. How far could they go before they needed a rest? How fast? There was no way they could get back home in one night, and they couldn't travel in broad daylight without being seen straight away. They would have to find places to hide during the day and only move during the hours of darkness. It would take days and days to get home! What would they eat?

What have I done? thought Petra. *I can't do this. I'll just have to get them out of here and then leave them. I'll have helped them to escape this horrible place. That's pretty good, isn't it? I can't be expected to get them all home as well. It will mean I won't get any credit for the rescue, but at least I'll get home and be safe and won't end up in there myself for the rest of my life.* Petra guiltily tried to stop the cowardly thoughts of abandoning the other dogs running through her mind. But she couldn't. Until the collie dog spoke up and interrupted them.

"Right then, Petra, it looks like those of us who can are ready to go. Lead us out of here."

"Oh, yes…right. It's this way," Petra gave the wretched boxer one last look before pushing through to the front of the dogs in the corridor. "Follow me."

"Not a sound," she warned them before they stepped out of the open door into the night. "There are two huge, evil guard dogs out here. They're asleep in their kennels, so you must be silent. If we wake them up, we'll never get out of here."

Nodding their understanding, the dogs held their breath as they padded quietly behind Petra.

Petra wasn't looking where she was going. She had her nose down to the ground, following her own scent trail to find her way back to the watery ditch. That was why she didn't see it. Just as she was about to lift her head and tell the other dogs she'd found their way out, a voice so close to her she jumped backwards snarled, "where do you think you're going?"

Petra looked up. Standing in front of their escape route was the grizzly bear guard dog. He towered above them like a dark shadow. All Petra could see was the glint of his eyes and the white of his bared teeth.

The way out was blocked. They were trapped.

TEN

Petra shrank back, away from the looming figure in front of her. She wished again that Lucy was with her. Lucy was never intimidated by other dogs. She'd have known what to say. Just as Petra was thinking this, the young Dalmatian in their pack stepped forward. She slunk on her belly, showing submission to the big dog.

"We just wanted to get out of here, out of that awful, dark stinky place, and this nice dog has come to help us. Would you step aside and let us out, please?" she asked bravely.

The guard dog softened slightly at the sight of the young Dalmatian, who was still a puppy really, but didn't move. "Afraid not. If you're in here, you belong to my humans. You're their property, and it's my job to make sure you stay inside the fence."

"What's going on here then, Buster?" The other, sandy-coloured dog, who looked like a lion, came rattling out of his kennel to join his companion. He plonked himself down for a scratch, jangling his collar and chain even more, then turned his giant face towards the cowering group in front of him. Even in the darkness, Petra could see his eyes were red-rimmed like the opening of a volcano.

"Sorry to wake you, Baxter," said Buster. "Caught these lot trying to escape. They're asking me to let them out. Can you believe it?"

Baxter turned his red eyes back to the group in front of him and cocked his head. "Why's that then?" he asked. "Why do you want out? Where do you want to go?"

"We want to go back home," said the husky, her voice shaking.

"Home? This is home," replied Baxter.

"No. It's not home for us. We've been taken from our homes. We want to get back to our humans," said the husky.

"Why?" asked Buster, looking puzzled.

"Because...it's not very nice here. Sorry, I know this is your home, but it's not a nice place. At my home, I get to sleep inside in a nice warm bed, and I get to play on the trampoline with my human friends and..."

"And I get to snuggle with my human in her bed, under the covers," the dachshund joined in.

"And we go everywhere with our human," Gomez piped up. "We're with her all day long: we even go to work with her. She'll be lost without us."

"Mine take me for walks all over the place, and they take me on holiday and give me nice food and cuddles and belly rubs," Petra joined in.

"What's a trampoline?" Buster asked.

"And what's a cuddle?" Baxter added.

"What's a cuddle? You mean you've never had a cuddle?" Petra was shocked that any dog could have never experienced a hug from a human and tried her best to explain it. It looked like these two dogs just lived their lives outside on chains, with only a kennel for shelter. They didn't get played with or walked or given treats or cuddles. They didn't know what any of it was. They were just here because they were scary and good at keeping people out. Maybe they weren't really bad dogs. Petra had an idea.

"Why don't you come with us?" she suggested nervously. "If you let us out, you could come with us. Maybe we could find you some humans who'll let you lie by the fire at night and groom you and take you out for walks in nice places and give you cuddles to show they love you."

The two big dogs looked at each other.

"We don't get any of that here," admitted Buster.

"Haven't been past that gate since I came here as a puppy," said Baxter. "I like the sound of cuddles. But we can't go."

"Why not?" asked Petra.

Baxter shook his head, and his collar and chain rattled in reply.

"I could help with that," the young Dalmatian volunteered. "I've still got some of my puppy teeth. They're very sharp, and they're driving me mad. I need something to chew on. I'll happily chew through that collar for you."

"Ohh, me too," said the dachshund. "I love to chew things up! I'll help."

And so, Buster and Baxter lay down so their necks could be reached, and bravely the two dogs set to work chewing. Baxter's collar was the first to fall as the

Dalmatian had the sharpest teeth. Petra and the husky also took a turn at helping to chew through Buster's collar, and soon, it too was lying on the ground with its chain still attached like a snake that had shed its skin.

"That feels so good," said Baxter, scratching where his collar had been.

"I feel so much lighter," said Buster, wagging his shaggy tail. "So, what now?"

The other dogs looked at the abandoned collars and were suddenly aware of the absence of their own. Removed and discarded by the thieves, the dogs felt bewildered. None of them had ever been outside without their collars on before.

"We go through there," said Petra, pointing to the ditch behind Buster.

"Through there?" said the greyhound, speaking for the first time. "But how? It's blocked."

"We have to go under the water. It's just for a second to get under the grille," Petra tried to reassure the greyhound, who looked stricken at the idea of covering herself in slimy water. "And there's no other way out. This is the only option we have."

Buster's tail stopped wagging, and he slumped to the ground. "Looks like we'll be staying here after all," he said to Baxter, dropping his head onto his paws.

"What? Why?" asked Petra.

"Never mind passing underneath the grille – we won't even fit in the ditch. It's only narrow. We're much too big."

Petra looked from the two guard dogs to the ditch and saw that Buster was right. The channel was much too narrow to fit dogs their size into it. That was probably why it hadn't been fully blocked up – it was far too small to be a possible escape route for the giant dogs.

Petra's shoulders sagged. It seemed such a terrible shame that they wouldn't be able to escape with the others and find a new life that didn't involve being permanently chained. These dogs didn't know love. They were just to keep people away from nosing into what might be inside the fence. But they weren't scary, really. They deserved better than this, but there was nothing she could do. She'd have to leave them behind.

Petra cleared her throat, ready to say goodbye and thank the big dogs for allowing them to escape, but she was interrupted by the husky.

"Ha, that's no problem," she said. "Leave this to me."

ELEVEN

Sunlight drizzled through the branches as morning arrived. After the husky had widened the ditch with some energetic digging, Buster and Baxter had been able to squeeze into it. Eventually, all of the dogs had dunked themselves under the grille and emerged on the other side. Invigorated by freedom, they'd travelled a couple of hours in what remained of the darkness, but soon, they were exhausted and needed to rest.

Petra had led them back the way she had come, following her own scent trail, but they hadn't got very far. Now they would have to hide in these woods during the day in case they were seen. The boxer's words hung in her mind like a mist she couldn't see through. All she could picture was the dog thieves finding them all while they slept and returning them back to the dark, smelly prison. They could end up being trapped in there for the rest of their lives. The thought of never being able to run free, or snuggle up on the sofa or play with Lucy ever again was too much for Petra to bear.

She led the band of weary dogs deep into the woods, looking for somewhere to hide. A fallen tree with a huge root seemed like the best place. The roots were covered in soil,grass and moss which provided an excellent screen to shield the dogs from anyone who might come looking for them.

"We'll rest here until it gets dark again," she said.

Gratefully the dogs flopped down into the hollow left by the tree's unearthed roots.

"We'll have to take turns to be on lookout duty," Petra said. "I'll go first. You all sleep."

The dogs didn't need to be told twice. They curled up together and closed their eyes. Petra noticed that the short-haired dogs who were feeling the chill from the early morning air, were snuggling up to Buster and

Baxter to keep warm. Only hours earlier, the two giant dogs had seemed like monsters, but now Petra could see how gentle they were. Gentle giants.

She placed her head on her paws, thinking. The pressure she felt from the dogs' hopes was enormous. They were looking at her to get them back to their families, and Petra didn't know if she could do it. The dream of flashing camera bulbs and people calling her name danced in her mind for a second. If she could do it, people would be so impressed. But what if she couldn't? Would leading them on take them into more danger? Would it be better for her to creep away and let them stay here? At least they were safe.

Petra couldn't decide what to do, and her eyelids felt heavy. *I have been awake a full day and night*, she said to herself. *I suppose a quick nap for a few minutes won't hurt...*

Petra was dreaming before she even realised she'd fallen asleep. In her dreams, the events of the previous day and night replayed. She pictured Lucy and the wasp; she felt stones under her feet and cold water on her skin as she relived her journey to the compound where the stolen dogs were. Her nostrils quivered as she recalled the stench of the building the dogs were held in, and her hackles rose as she pictured the boxer's sad face and her warning that the thieves would be looking for them. Her heart weighed heavy at the memory of having to leave Buster and Baxter behind, but then her tail thumped on the ground as she pictured the husky frantically digging in the ditch to make it wide enough for them to fit into. The husky was an expert digger, as was the little dachshund who soon joined in. In no time, all of the dogs were digging, and they were out!

The greyhound and dachshund hadn't been at all keen on the slimy water in the ditch and had practically had to be pushed in to get them to the other side. They'd all emerged from the ditch slippery and mucky, but they were free! To start with, that had given them the energy to move quickly, but the pace had soon slowed. Poor Gizmo never complained, but her twisted leg meant that she just couldn't move quickly. With his flat face, Gomez was soon out of breath and wheezing as if his lungs might burst. Though tired and hungry, the other dogs could probably have travelled a bit further, but Gomez and Gizmo could not. And so, they'd stopped in this wood.

When Petra's eyes opened again, she knew immediately that something was wrong. Her stomach was hollow with hunger, but that wasn't it. The sun was in a different position in the sky. *Oh no! I've slept too long. It's late in the afternoon,* Petra thought, realising that she'd missed her chance to slip away.

Although that idea dismayed her, she knew it wasn't the reason she felt sick. She looked at the bundle of sleeping dogs. Some were starting to wake up. They were yawning and stretching. What was it that was wrong?

Petra counted the dogs slowly. Then she counted them again and again, hoping she was wrong. But each time she counted them, there were only eight. There should be nine. Who was missing? The Dalmatian stood out a mile with her striking black and white markings, but the other dogs were all shades of brown, black and grey and mingled together like a patchwork quilt. Buster and Baxter were still there. They were easy to spot because of their size. Gomez, the pug, was snoring his head off, and Gizmo was right beside him. She could make out the long black body of the dachshund and the long grey legs of the greyhound. The border collie was getting to her feet and stretching so that only left... the husky!

"The husky is missing!" Petra whimpered. "The thieves must have been and taken her!"

The collie was barely awake, but she was instantly alert. With no trace of panic, she said, "don't be silly. If the thieves had found us, they'd have taken all of us, not just one. She'll just have wandered off. I'll find her and fetch her back."

Feeling slightly calmer since the collie had taken control of the missing dog situation, Petra prepared to explain what was happening to the rest of the group as they were all waking up. Once the initial panic was over, thoughts turned to food. Every dog was starving hungry.

"How long do you think it will take us to get home?" the greyhound asked.

Petra didn't know where these dogs' homes were, but she knew that going at the slow pace of Gomez and

Gizmo would mean it could take days to get back to her home.

"Erm, a few days possibly?" she ventured.

"A few *days*? What are we supposed to do about food until then? We're hungry now!" said Gomez, who loved his food and was used to regular, quality meals from the vet. "We can't go without dinner for days."

"I know!" said the greyhound, her eyes gleaming. "I'll hunt for rabbits. At the race track, we run after a rabbit, but it always gets away. Maybe wild, woodland rabbits will be fat and slow. I'll be able to get us some to eat."

"Oh, yes – me too!" said the dachshund, who was always keen to get involved in everything. "I can hunt. I'm very good at catching moles and mice."

"Hold on. You expect us to eat...animals? With fur on?" said Gomez, aghast. He pictured his little foil tins with the peel back lids that revealed succulent cuts of meat with delicious gravy.

"You eat meat, don't you? Where do you think it comes from?" the dachshund scoffed. "If you don't want to starve, you'll have to eat what we can find. My ancestors were bred to hunt, as were greyhounds and pointers. We need to eat to survive. Are you coming with us, Petra?"

Petra paused. The dachshund's words made her realise why she couldn't stay with Lucy and the Daleys on walks and why she was always drawn away from them into the woods. She'd been bred to hunt. It was programmed into her. But although she loved searching for rabbits, pheasants and deer, and loved chasing them, it was just for fun. She had no intention of catching them. There was no need as the Daleys always gave her plenty of good food. But now, faced with nothing to eat for days, could she do it? Could she

hunt for real? It was time to find out.

TWELVE

As the collie suspected, the husky hadn't been stolen. She'd just wandered off and had a little adventure on her own, following the scent of a squirrel until it came to an end at a tree. The collie had found the wolf-like dog staring up into the branches and escorted her back to rejoin the group.

When they returned, the sheep dog assumed control of the group. Her first task was to divide the food up. Petra, the greyhound and the dachshund had caught a pheasant, a rabbit, two moles and five mice between them. It wasn't much to split between ten dogs, especially when two of them were more than twice the size of anyone else, but it was better than nothing.

Once they'd all eaten and felt a little better, the collie jumped up on a rock and introduced herself. "I'm

Pepper," she said, "and I'm used to having a job to do. I know that Petra here is our leader and captain, but I'd like to put myself forward as sergeant, if no-one has any objections?"

The other dogs looked at each other and shook their heads. Petra sat up a little straighter at being called their leader and captain.

"Good. Well, first I think we need a little organisation, starting with some introductions. I was taken early one morning while I was out on my lands, checking for sheep that might have got themselves stuck on their backs or in the fences. Because I was concentrating on my job, I didn't notice there was someone behind me. Two big men grabbed me and flung me into the back of a van. It seems like a long time ago, but it might only have happened a few days ago. What about the rest of you? What are your names, and what happened to you?"

Each dog took its turn. Gomez spoke first, for himself and Gizmo, explaining how the vet always let the two of them out into the little garden at her surgery around dinner time. She usually sat outside with them while she ate her lunch, but the phone had rung. No-one was answering it, so she'd dashed in to pick it up. No sooner had she gone back into the building than two men had darted out of a van parked opposite the garden, scooped the dogs up and driven off with them.

The stories continued. The husky went next.

"I'm Storm," she said. "I was out in the garden too. I'd been playing on the trampoline with my little humans. After a while, they'd got bored of it and got down, but they had no shoes on. The boy stood on a sharp stone and cut his foot, so they all went racing back in the house to stop him bleeding, and I was left on my own. Well, then a cat came into the garden. It saw me, lying on the trampoline and streaked off, jumping right over the fence into next door's garden. I chased it, but I couldn't get over the fence. So, I dug under it and squeezed through. There was no sign of the cat by then, but I decided to go and do some exploring by myself while I was at a loose end. I was just trotting down the street towards the smell of cooking sausages coming from another garden when I felt someone seize my collar. The next thing I knew, I was in a cage in the dark."

The dachshund was Sprite. She'd been snatched while on a walk. She'd gone into some bushes to have a private wee while her humans continued walking along the park path and been grabbed by rough hands and bundled into a crate.

The greyhound was Dusty – aptly named as her coat was the colour of dust. She'd been taken out of her owner's van at the racetrack while her humans were watching their other dog race. She'd come second in her race that day and was resting in her crate. When the doors had opened, she'd thought it was her humans returning with Bobby, the other dog. But it wasn't. She'd frozen and pressed herself as far back in her crate as she could go, but the man had just reached in and roughly pulled her out. She'd been thrown into the back of a different van and driven away.

Buster hadn't been stolen. He'd been brought to the compound as a puppy and been kept outside on a chain from the beginning. He couldn't remember anything before that. A year later, another puppy – Baxter – had been brought to join him. They'd grown up together but had been nowhere, done nothing, had no adventures together.

"I'm a bit peckish, but I'm enjoying being out in the open with all of you," said Baxter.

"Yes, it's like having friends," said Buster. "It's nice to get to know you all."

Finally, the Dalmatian came forward. She was the youngest of the group but she spoke confidently. "I'm Bluebell," she said, "but everyone calls me Bella for short. I was taken out of the garden too." She shuddered as she remembered. "I spent a lot of time in the garden on my own. When my humans first brought me home, they loved me and said how cute I was. But when I went to the toilet on their carpets, they shouted and threw me out into the garden for hours. As I got bigger, my teeth started to hurt. I needed to chew to stop them aching, so I chewed whatever I could find. This made them shout even more, and soon I was out in the garden on my own every day for hours. I got lonely and cold, so I'd bark. One day, a man came to the garden fence and spoke to me. He had some food, so I went to see what it was. He opened the gate and gave me the food. I thought he was nice as he gave me lots of pats and attention as well. Then he put a lead on my collar and walked me out, and put me in the back of a van or something. It smelled of dogs, so I thought I was being taken to a nice place where there'd be other dogs to play with, but then I ended up at *that* place. It was far worse than where I'd been before."

Petra felt awful. Some of the dogs had nice homes that, like her, they wanted to get back to, but not all of them. Buster, Baxter and Bella had unhappy lives. What would happen to them when this was over?

"Good," said Pepper. Now we all know each other, it's time to get going again. Petra is going to lead us. I suggest that Dusty, you go at the back and be the lookout. You can stay behind us and keep an eye out for the bad men following us. If you see them, you can sprint up to warn us, and we can look for somewhere to hide. My job is going to be to stop Storm from wandering off."

"Sorry," said Storm. "I'll try to concentrate, but I just get so easily distracted."

"I'll be keeping an eye on you," promised Pepper. "Boys," she said, addressing the mastiffs, you're our guards. You can position yourselves on the outside of the group, and perhaps you might also offer some assistance to those of us who need it."

"What do you mean?" asked Buster.

"Perhaps you'd let our short-legged companions ride on your backs?" Pepper asked, looking at Gomez, Gizmo and Sprite.

"Excuse me! I don't need to be carried!" exclaimed Sprite, indignantly. "I've done all the Wainwrights, you know!"

"Fine, not you then," sighed Pepper. "But perhaps you two would appreciate a lift?" she asked Gomez and Gizmo.

The two dogs were reluctant to hitch a lift on the backs of Buster and Baxter, but the boys immediately agreed, pleased to have a job to do in Pepper's squad. The two smaller dogs felt that they had to accept. They didn't want to turn down the generous offer or slow the pack as they tried to head towards safety. But both of them secretly hoped they would get a chance to be helpful during the journey as every other dog seemed to have a purpose.

Pepper and Petra pushed Gomez and Gizmo onto the backs of their transport.

"I think we're ready to move off," said Sergeant Pepper. All of the dogs blended in with the dark shadows of the evening – except Bella. Her white coat gleamed so brightly in the moonlight, she looked luminous. "Positions, please. Keep your eyes open for a patch of mud. This Dalmatian needs a disguise. All ready? Then let's move off. Follow Petra!"

As the sun slipped away, pulling down a blind of darkness in its wake, it was time for the dogs to move on. With slightly less empty bellies, they crept out of the woods and into the fields that lay beyond.

THIRTEEN

Pepper's military manoeuvre didn't last long. Gomez and Gizmo kept slipping off the mastiffs' backs and ended up having to walk. Storm was forever drifting off and having to be rounded up. Dusty was too nervous about being at the back on her own, so she gave up on being the back-stop lookout, and Buster and Baxter soon started to flag. Because they never did any exercise, they were both terribly unfit. When Petra's route led them to a five-barred gate in the field they were crossing, they all stopped, assuming they could go no further.

Unaware that her companions had pulled up, Petra quickly scaled the gate. She was up and over in a matter of seconds. On the other side, she peered through the bars of the gate at the other dogs, realising that they could not climb over

"That's a pretty unique skill you've got there, Petra," said Dusty. "I don't think any of us could even attempt it."

They're all stuck. They can't follow, thought Petra, looking through the gate at the trapped dogs. *The thieves might not be far behind us. What should I do?* She looked longingly over her shoulder at the way home and almost went for it. But when she turned back to give her companions one last look, Gomez's eyes stilled her. He was peering intently at her. He didn't make a sound, but Petra heard the words, "don't leave us," as clear as day. The other dogs were looking at her in awe and admiration. How could she turn her back on them and leave them to fend for themselves?

"Storm, it's time to get digging," Gomez said, indicating that the husky should use her brilliant tunnelling skills to dig a route under the gate.

"Yes!" cried Storm, pleased to be of service.

"Me too!" said Sprite.

Clods of earth flew through the air as the dogs dug under the gate. Petra abandoned her thoughts of running away and joined in from her side. As soon as she was able, Sprite squeezed under to Petra's side and helped her. Eventually, the tunnel was deep enough even for Buster and Baxter to pass through it but it had wasted a lot of time and energy. The pace became desperately slow.

The next obstacle they were faced with was the lake Petra had swum across on her outbound journey. Moonlight glinted off the water's still surface, making it look as cold as Petra knew it would be. The dogs lined up along the water's edge, staring out at the expanse of dark water ahead of them.

"You cannot be serious," said Gomez. "There's no way we can go across there. I'll drown! We have to find a way round."

Petra looked up and down the length of the lake. "But it goes on forever. To go round it would take us *miles* out of our way. Plus, I don't know that way. I came across the water. One way or another, we have to get across."

"Let's sleep on it, suggested Pepper. We can rest in the woods over there and decide what to do."

"But there's hours left until morning," Petra protested. "We can't stop already. We've hardly covered any distance."

"Yes, but not every dog is as fit and agile as you and I," she said, looking at Buster, Baxter, Gomez, Gizmo and young Bella. They were all swaying with weariness. Pepper lowered her voice. "We have to move at the pace of the slowest member of the team."

Petra clenched her teeth in frustration. The collie was used to herding sheep and having to wait for them to move, but she wasn't. She never waited for anyone.

Pepper called them a *team*. If they were a team, every dog would be pulling their weight and finding a way to be useful, but they weren't. Some of these dogs were holding the team back.

"Come on," said Pepper, sensing Petra's irritation. "We haven't had much to eat. Let's find a place to shelter. Then you, Dusty and Sprite can go and hunt. Once we've eaten, we'll come up with a plan to cross the lake tomorrow."

Reluctantly, Petra set off with Dusty and Sprite to hunt while the other dogs looked for a place to shelter. When she returned later with a rabbit she'd caught, she followed their scent to an old tunnel in the woods. The entrance was obscured by boulders stacked in front of it, and the other side was blocked by trees and brambles. She could see how the smaller dogs had managed to squeeze in, but she wondered how Buster and Baxter had fit between the gaps in the rocks. It was an excellent hiding place, she had to admit, though she was still frustrated by how little they had travelled that night.

Inside the tunnel, she dropped the rabbit she'd brought and was surprised to see a stash of other food items sitting there untouched. There were two other rabbits and several mice plus a range of human food: half-eaten apples, bread crusts, a couple of squashed pies, some cheese and a few mini sausages.

"Gomez and Gizmo found these," Bella informed her. "They'd been left on the shores by picnickers, so they brought them all back here."

Petra was shocked. To bring all of that back to the tunnel would have needed several trips. The two little dogs had clearly worked very hard at their task.

"And I found this," Bella said, pushing forward a strange board on wheels.

"What's that?" asked Petra, puzzled. It certainly wasn't something to eat.

"That's a skateboard," said Storm, explaining how humans used skateboards.

"I thought…" said Bella, "for Gomez and Gizmo. They can sit on it and be pulled along."

"That's going to be my job," said Storm, puffing her chest out with pride.

"We'll show you," said Pepper, seeing Petra's confusion.

Back outside the tunnel, Pepper showed Petra how a rope she'd found had been tied at both ends around the metal plate the skateboard's front wheels were attached to. Storm picked up the rope in her mouth, Gomez and Gizmo climbed onto the deck, and Storm pulled them forward.

Petra wagged her tail. She was impressed and could sense that the other dogs were desperate for her approval – it made her feel important. Her wagging tail brushed all of her grumpiness away. Maybe this could work after all. Maybe she could get them all home. Maybe they could work as a team to find solutions to all the problems they faced. There was still one problem she couldn't see a way around, though.

The lake.

FOURTEEN

After the food was divided up and eaten, the dogs discussed the lake problem. It seemed the only confident swimmers were Petra and Pepper. Most of the dogs had never attempted to swim before and were nervous about trying to cross a lake on their first effort. There was nowhere to stop for a rest on the way; the crossing had to be made in one go. Bella was willing to give it a try, and Dusty said she would too if she absolutely had to, though she was more worried about freezing to death than drowning, since her coat was so thin. She'd already torn her skin in several places from chasing rabbits into brambles and some of her wounds were bleeding. Gizmo had taken it upon herself to pull out any remaining bramble thorns from Dusty's skin and lick her wounds clean. She and Gomez could not swim at all, and Sprite would soon be exhausted trying to doggy paddle across the lake with her short legs.

Buster and Baxter were too heavy, and their thick coats would get waterlogged and make them sink. Lastly, Storm had an absolute phobia of water, which, she said, came from her ancestors.

"Where they lived, it was so cold that everywhere was covered in ice and snow. If the ice broke, the water under it was so freezing it would kill any dog who fell in. Now all huskies are born to not trust water. It's a survival instinct," she explained.

With only two out of ten dogs being good swimmers, it looked impossible to find a way to get them across. Pepper advised them to sleep on it, and hopefully, they might have an idea when they were rested. So most of the dogs slept the day away, only being woken occasionally by Gomez's snores and pumps.

"Eww, Gomez, you stink," Bella said, wrinkling her nose.

"Sorry, but you can't talk. You might think you're posh, Lady Bluebell, but you're full of wind too. And your pumps aren't just smelly; they're squeaky as well!"

"They are not," said Bella, embarrassed. She'd hoped that the others would think her accidental pumps were coming from Gomez, but now he'd told everyone her secret.

As they drifted off back to sleep, Pepper remained awake. Someone needed to come up with a plan to get them across the lake. It was a similar idea to herding sheep: they all needed to cross at the same time and stay together. It would be no good if any dog drifted off or got left behind. But how could that be achieved when most of them couldn't even swim at all?

Pepper crept out of the tunnel and crawled to the water's edge. The sun was out, and lots of humans were playing in the lake. She watched them with interest. Some were paddling, some were swimming, and some were rowing around on boats and kayaks using oars or paddles to pull themselves through the water.

I've got it, she thought, wagging her tail. With that, she went back to the tunnel to sleep, content that she now knew how to get every dog safely across the lake.

***

"You're a genius," said Petra later when Pepper took her to one side, "if it works. Do you think it will work?"

"I don't think there's any other way," said Pepper. "I'm sure that between us, we can get them all across. Like you said, it's either that or a detour of miles and miles."

"You're right. We have to try."

When it was dark again, and all the humans had gone, Pepper escorted the dogs down to the lakeshore, where they cleared up the last scraps left from the picnickers. Storm pulled the skateboard, but Gomez and Gizmo were soon shaken off as their route was full of bumpy tree roots. It wasn't far from the tunnel to the water's edge, so they opted to walk.

"Here we are," said Pepper, leading them to a line of rowing boats that were lying on the stony beach. "This is how we're getting you across. You're all going in the boat, and Petra and I are going to swim behind and push it."

Every dog thought this was an excellent idea, and after loading the skateboard into the boat, they all climbed in, eager to get started. But there was another problem. Petra and Pepper couldn't get the boat to move when they tried to push it into the water.

"Everyone out," said Petra. Then they tried again to push the now empty boat. It was still too heavy for them to move.

"At last," said Buster. "We haven't been able to do much to help yet, but I think this is where Baxter and I come in. Come on big lad, let's get this thing moving."

Buster went to the front of the boat, where a rope was attached to the bow. He took it in his mouth and pulled while Baxter put all his weight against the back and pushed. It took all of their strength to inch the boat forward over the stones. Seeing them struggling, the other dogs all joined in, putting their shoulders against any part of the boat they could reach to help Baxter push. Eventually, it gained momentum, and they heard a little splash as it met the water. The bigger dogs helped the smaller ones into the boat. Baxter was last to get in and nearly capsized it as he pulled himself over the side. The boat rocked dangerously before it settled and sat still, waiting to be propelled to the other side.

Petra and Pepper stepped gingerly into the water, the cold biting their paws and taking their breath away. But they pressed on, pushing their shoulders against the hull. Soon there were no stones under their paws anymore, and they were swimming, slowly guiding their warm, dry passengers across the lake.

"A little to the left! We're drifting right," called Bella, who had placed herself as a lookout at the front of the boat. Although it was dark, her keen eyes could make out land and the quickest way to reach it.

"To the left," the message got passed along the boat and down to Pepper, who was swimming on its right side.

"Give it a bit of a nudge, Pepper," called Gomez. "Bella is guiding us across the narrowest part of the lake."

Thanks to Bella's consideration, they made it. Petra and Pepper couldn't have swum any further. The inky water was so cold, they were both numb when they dragged themselves onto the opposite shore. After they'd shaken the worst of the water from their coats, the other dogs surrounded them and pressed themselves up against the wet fur of the swimmers, helping to warm and dry them. Both dogs would have liked to rest, but they were so cold, they knew the best thing was to keep moving. So, loading Gomez and Gizmo onto their skateboard sledge, the dogs followed Petra as she led them home, leaving the black lake behind them.

What they didn't see in their hurry to get on their way was a young man standing a little way away from them, blocked by a tree on the shore. He was blinking and shaking his head, wondering if he was dreaming, or if he'd had too much to drink at the pub. He'd just witnessed a boatload of dogs crossing the lake in what appeared to be a magically moving boat. And then, two of them had mounted a skateboard and been pulled away by a husky. It couldn't be true. But when he checked his phone and watched the video he'd just shot, it was all there.

He wasn't dreaming. It was real.

FIFTEEN

That night the dogs travelled their furthest distance. It still wasn't far by Petra's standards, but it was an improvement. Petra and Pepper were tired from their swim, but kept moving to keep warm. Storm was more mindful of where she was going and took care to choose the smoothest path, avoiding lumps and bumps that would bounce her passengers off the skateboard. Since she'd been given a job and something to concentrate on, she hadn't tried to wander off once.

When they arrived at fences that Petra could jump or gates that Petra could climb, and the other dogs were stuck, Pepper became an expert at finding gaps in hedges and areas of loose fencing. Buster and Baxter were usually too big to fit through these gaps, but it required less digging to get them through.

They all felt a great sense of achievement and teamwork by the time the sun started to rise, and they took shelter in a cave. They snuggled up close together for warmth and fell asleep immediately, despite their rumbling tummies.

Sometime in the early afternoon, they were woken by the sound of rain battering the rocks around them. The downpour lasted for hours. The dogs were grateful to be warm, dry and cosy and went back to sleep. By the time Petra and Pepper woke in the late afternoon, they were amazed to see a pile of food in the middle of the cave. Clearly, they'd slept longer than the others. There were two rabbits from Dusty, four moles from Sprite and, Petra was surprised to see a large pheasant.

"Found it lying on the road nearby. Hit by a car," explained Storm. "It seemed a waste to leave it there."

It sounded like Storm had been off wandering again while Pepper was asleep.

There were also three large fish on the pile. "That was us," said Baxter happily. "We found a river and waded in. I got two, and Buster got one. They were near the edge, hiding under tree roots. There were more, but the rest swam away when we got close. We managed to grab these, though."

Gomez was still missing his gourmet meals, but he found that he enjoyed the fish and complained less about having to live like a wild dog.

By the time they'd all eaten their fill, it was almost time to set off again. Petra reckoned they were just under halfway. Although they'd speeded up slightly and were becoming a better team, each dog doing whatever it could to help the group, there was still a long way to go. There was still a mountain to go over. Petra's scent trail was weakening as it was now three days old, but she could remember the way. The mountain was high, and the path was rough. How were the mastiffs going to cope? What about Gomez and Gizmo? She couldn't see the skateboard travelling over some of the rocky crags. Maybe they'd have to find a way round the mountain, rather than over it. But she didn't know that way.

Where was the wasp? Why hadn't he come back to check on them and see if they needed any more help? *Some 'guide' he was,* Petra thought. *He's just abandoned us. What a great friend,* she added sarcastically. It was going to be up to her to decide what to do. The responsibility weighed heavily on her as she knew that the other dogs trusted her and would follow her wherever she took them. Was it best to take them a way she knew would be horribly difficult for them, a way where there was no shelter at all from the cold? Or should she try to find an easier route? Going round the mountain would be flatter, but much further, and she'd just have to guess where to go. It would take them even longer to get home if they went a different way. Plus, they could end up running into people if the new route took them to places where there were houses.

The other dogs were waiting for her to lead them. Petra didn't know what to do.

"Hey, Bella," she said, stalling for time, "now it's rained, there's bound to be some mud nearby. Keep an eye out and if you spot any, jump in. You need to be better camouflaged."

"Ha ha, if I *spot* any. Very funny, Petra," giggled the puppy.

As the dogs set off in the direction of the mountain, Petra watched the others. Pepper had gone to the back of the group to keep an eye on everyone and make sure no dog got left behind. Also near the back were the big dogs who walked very slowly, and surprisingly, Dusty the greyhound. Petra had been shocked to learn that the greyhound was only used to sprinting a few minutes each day. The rest of the time, she admitted, she was pretty lazy and liked an easy life relaxing with Bobby, her kennel mate. In front of them was Storm. She was taking her time to go as gently as possible so as not to tip the skateboard. Gomez and Gizmo took turns walking beside the husky, so she didn't have to pull them both along all the time. When the one walking got tired, they'd swap. Sprite and Bella were always at the front near her. Bella loved to keep up with the leader and trotted along with her head and tail held high. It was quite sad really that this was the highlight of the young dog's life so far. She'd had no-one to play with her before. She'd just been ignored. Now she had company. Petra could see Bella smiling as she looked across at her and her heart ached. It was awful to think that the pup probably didn't have a family who were desperately missing her, like she knew hers would be. Bella made her think of Lucy, and she missed her best friend.

I'll see her again soon, Petra said to herself as she led the group across the field.

SIXTEEN

When the dogs reached the base of the mountain, Petra decided to take them around it instead of over it. Not knowing which direction would be best, she opted to go left. Left meant west, and she knew that home was in that direction. But she had no idea where she was leading them to. Her tension and worry hung over her like a dark cloud, and soon the other dogs could feel its presence. Gomez tried to lighten the mood by telling jokes.

"Hey Pepper," called Gomez. "What do you get if you cross a sheepdog with a daffodil? A collie-flower! Bella, what did the hungry Dalmatian say after her meal? That hit the spot!"

"Gomez, what does your human do when she's finished giving you a bath?" Bella joined in. "She pulls the pug out!"

"If any dog needs a bath, it's you. You're filthy."

"Thank you," said Bella. In one of the fields they'd crossed, there had been a wet, boggy patch. They'd had to go around it to stop the skateboard from sinking in the mud, but Bella had seen it as her opportunity to follow Petra's command and disguise herself. She'd thrown herself in with enthusiasm and rolled around in the bog until every inch of her was covered in dark, wet mud.

"Look at me!" she'd said to Petra, "no-one can tell I'm a Dalmatian now."

"No, they certainly can't," Petra agreed in disbelief. She'd never seen Lucy with even a speck of dirt on her. She always managed to keep herself spotlessly clean. But this Dalmatian clearly didn't mind being completely filthy, never mind a little bit mucky.

"Why is a dog like a big tree?" Gomez resumed his joke-telling. "Both have lots of bark!"

"Shush a minute," said Pepper from the back of the group. "What's that strange noise?"

The dogs pulled up and listened. They could hear a faint whirring sound. It seemed to be coming from the sky above them.

Is it the wasps? Petra wondered. *Have they come back to show us the right way to go?*

But it wasn't a swarm of wasps; it wasn't a bird; it was a strange white object hovering above them. It looked like it was watching them.

"What is it?" asked Dusty.

"It looks like some sort of machine," said Storm, who seemed to know the most about human contraptions.

"I don't like it," said Pepper. "Come on, keep moving."

Petra's hackles rose as the strange, white object continued to follow them. What was it? What did it want? Just as she was about to snap, it rose up into the sky, out of sight and disappeared.

"Thank dog for that," she said. "It was getting on my nerves."

Petra's relief that the flying object had left them soon disappeared. The track they were following downhill came out at a narrow country road. Nearby she could see a cluster of houses. As she'd feared, she'd led them to a village.

"Oh no. Houses," she said to the others. "We'll have to look for a way to get back into a field to keep away from them."

She was met with groans. "Please, Petra, can we stay on the road for a while?" begged Sprite. "It's so lovely and flat and smooth."

Petra knew that the off-road routes were tiring for the other dogs, but they were necessary for safety. She pointed this out to them.

"But there's no lights on," said Gizmo. "The humans will all be in bed sleeping. No-one will see us."

Nine pairs of eyes pleaded with her. She hesitated but couldn't bring herself to resist them.

"Okay," she agreed, stepping forward on the tarmac road.

The group crept through the village. Every dog was alert for any sound or sight of humans, but there were none. No curtains twitched; no cars came. As Gizmo said, the humans were fast asleep.

Stealing carefully through the silent village took some time, but at last, they were past the houses and on the other side.

"Phew, we made it," sighed Petra. "Nobody saw us."

"Remind me...why are we so worried about being seen?" Buster asked.

"We don't know who we can trust. If we're seen, the thieves could find out where we are. Humans have those telephone things, and they can get messages to each other as quick as blinking. We've got to stay out of sight until we get back to my home. My humans will know what to do."

The dogs continued walking along the road until Pepper's sensitive ears heard another noise.

"Something's coming," she said.

As soon as the words were out of her mouth, the dogs could see headlights bouncing towards them as a vehicle travelled along the twisty road in their direction.

"Quick! We have to get off the road and hide," Petra commanded. "Run!"

She ran towards a pair of stone gate stoops further up the road on their left. Thankfully the gateway was open as the gate lay rotten in the grass, half-grown over.

"Up there," she said, spying an old shepherd's hut. "We'll get in there and hide.

Dusty overtook them and was the first one into the shelter, followed by Petra and Bella. Storm would've been next, but the skateboard had gotten stuck in the gate's rungs, meaning it had to be left there. She and Pepper were helping Gomez and Gizmo up the hill. Sprite arrived with Buster and Baxter, but the other four still hadn't made it as the headlights neared the gateway.

Storm's white tail was lit up like a strike of lightning as the van pulled to a halt in the gateway.

"What are they doing? Why have they stopped?" Bella whimpered. The thud of doors opening and closing could be heard. The first glimmer of sunlight appeared, and in the grey dawn, Petra could make out the shape of two men coming up the hill behind Gomez, Gizmo, Pepper and Storm.

"It's them," said Baxter, recognising the men's outlines. "They've found us."

SEVENTEEN

"We need to stop them! They're going to grab Pepper!" Buster cried. Even though Pepper could easily have ran up the hill away from the thieves, she wouldn't leave Gomez and Gizmo. Neither would Storm, who'd become very protective of her two little passengers. Watching the two small dogs struggle up the hill was unbearable for them all.

"Yes, let's go and get them," snarled Sprite.

"No, you lot stay back," said Buster. We'll handle this."

Petra, Bella, Sprite and Dusty stood in the doorway of the shepherd's hut as Buster and Baxter went out to meet the men who'd chained them for their whole lives.

For the first time since they'd left the compound, the big dogs barked. The sound boomed like cannons firing. The thieves paused, looking up the hillside towards the sound. The four dogs they were chasing didn't stop. They kept moving. Buster and Baxter came forward to meet them.

"Quick, get behind us," Baxter told them.

With one last giant effort, Gomez, Gizmo, Storm and Pepper managed to reach their guardians. The big dogs stood between them and the men. Gone were the big softies the other dogs had come to know them as. Their faces were arranged into snarls, their huge sharp teeth ready to bite. Baxter's red eyes blazed in fury as the men spoke to them.

"Boys, come on, it's us," one of the men said, not daring to come any closer. "See what we've brought for you." He pulled two enormous slabs of steak out of a rucksack and threw them at the dogs' feet. The mastiffs didn't even look at the offering. They could sense the bad intentions of these men, like static electricity in the air. They stood their ground, continuing to snarl and bark.

"Go, get them back to the others," Buster growled at Storm.

Reluctantly, Storm and Pepper ushered Gomez and Gizmo up the hill to where the other pack members were watching in horror.

"No," barked Petra, just as they reached the hut. They all turned in time to see what Petra and the other dogs were witnessing.

Both men had pulled a rope with looped ends out of their rucksacks. The men had thrown the loops over the heads of Buster and Baxter like a lasso and were pulling with all their might.

"Come *on*," said the man with a beard. "You're coming home with us. Move."

The dogs dug their heels in and attempted to reverse away from their captors. But as they pulled back, the ropes tightened around their necks, strangling them. Buster and Baxter resisted for as long as they could, but they couldn't breathe with the ropes biting into their throats. They were forced to step forward. As soon as they moved, the men yanked on the ropes, dragging the dogs towards them. They continued to struggle but every time they did, the ropes tightened again and they had to move. Slowly, the men were succeeding in hauling Buster and Baxter down the hill.

"They're going to put them in their van," said Pepper, seeing the red van parked in the open gateway of the field, "then they'll be coming back for us."

"We could run for it?" said Dusty.

"Not all of us can," said Storm, looking sorrowfully at the skateboard riders.

"Don't stay and get caught because of us," said Gizmo sadly, nudging her head against Storm's side. "You can all get away. Thank you for all you've done, but go. Save yourselves."

Petra's legs trembled. There had been a time when that was all she wanted. To save herself and get home. There was no way she could face a life of captivity, held prisoner in a cage forever, never seeing her family again. But now, although it looked like that was exactly what was going to happen, she found she couldn't abandon the other dogs. They were her friends.

She looked at them: Dusty - chief rabbit catcher, Sprite – mole hunter and tunnel digger, Gomez – noisy snorer and comedian, Gizmo – the kind one, Buster and Baxter – fish catchers, and protectors, Storm – tunnel digger and sledge puller, Bella – always happy and uncomplaining, and Pepper – the clever one. The one who looked after every dog and made sure they all stayed together. How could she leave them now? How could she ever have considered it?

At first, all she'd seen were their faults and the way they couldn't do what she could do. She'd just seen that they were a nuisance who held her back. Now she realised they all had strengths too. They'd worked together to solve problems. Yes, she could have gotten home quicker if she'd left them, but Petra was glad she hadn't. They'd taught her a few things about herself that she hadn't thought about before, and if she ever got out of this mess, she'd try to be a better dog: less impatient, more thoughtful, and she'd stop having jealous thoughts about all the attention Lucy got. Petra could see now that her friend thoroughly deserved it after all she'd gone through.

Unable to bear the sadness welling inside her, Petra put her head back and howled. She howled for Buster and Baxter, who'd allowed them all to escape and were now being dragged back to hell. She howled

for herself and the other dogs, who would shortly be in

cages for the rest of their lives. She howled for Lucy

and the Daleys, who would never know where she was

and what had happened to her.

Bella joined her. Her howl was thin and puppy-like but still full of emotion. Then Pepper and Dusty, Gomez and Gizmo and Sprite joined in. Their howls harmonised together in a melody of misery. Finally, Storm added her voice. She looked like a wolf howling at the rising sun.

Her howl was long and deep and primitive. It made a shiver run through the pack. It was a call that connected them in some magical way. They felt like they could feel each other's heartbeats and read each other's minds. Even Buster and Baxter stopped wrestling against the ropes and started to howl.

And then something happened.

EIGHTEEN

At first, Petra thought the weird flying object from earlier had returned. She could hear the same sort of whirring in the air. But then it got louder and louder. It wasn't whirring. It was buzzing. It was wasps. A whole swarm of them!

What are they doing? Petra wondered. *Why have they come now? They're too late to help now! They should have come before, when I didn't know which way to go. It's my fault this is happening – I led us into this place where there are people. The wasps could have shown us a different way.*

The dogs looked on in surprise as the wasps made a ring around Buster and Baxter and the thieves, surrounding them. There was no way out.

"Aaarrghh, I hate wasps," said the taller of the two men, wafting his arms around, swatting at them.

"Don't do that," said the bearded one. "You'll make 'em angry."

As some of the wasps were whacked by the man's flailing arms, they did indeed get angry. The buzzing got louder, and the attack began.

Soon, the men had dropped the ropes and were running back down the hill, covering their heads with their arms as the wasps looked for skin to sting.

"Aaaaarrrrgggggghhhh! Stop it, stop it!" they both screamed as they stumbled and tripped their way back to their van.

Once the men had jumped in and slammed the van doors, the dogs cheered the wasps as they flew away.

"Thank you. Thank you so much!" they called to the swarm, but the wasps didn't stay to listen. Soon they were all gone.

"That was amazing."

"Where did they come from?"

"Why did they help us?"

The dogs were full of questions. Petra remembered Lucy telling her how the wasps helped to point out where she went missing by forming a giant arrow in the air. *They're like mini superheroes,* she thought. *Turning up to help in the nick of time just when they're needed.*

"Maybe they heard our howling?" Storm said.

Buster and Baxter rejoined them just as the van's engine sounded. But the men found that they couldn't get away. They were blocked in on either side by other cars.

"Oi, get your cars out of the way now!" the bearded man jumped out and was shouting at the drivers of the cars.

One of them put his window down to show that he was on the phone. He spoke loudly to let the man know who he was talking to. With their excellent hearing, the dogs heard it too. "Police? Yes, I've found the dog thieves that have been all over the news this week. Where are they? They're at...wait! They've run off!

They've jumped out of the van and are running away across the fields."

The dogs watched them go. They knew that the thieves would leave them alone now. They'd only be interested in saving their own skins and avoiding the police. Otherwise, they'd be spending some time in cages themselves.

It was fully daylight by now. With Buster and Baxter safely back with them, the dogs retreated into the shepherd's hut and curled up. After all the events of that night, they were dog tired. Sunlight shone through the broken roof and landed on them like a warm blanket. They felt so cosy and relieved to be all together again, they were fast asleep in seconds.

In no time at all, they were being woken up again. They were surrounded by people wearing black uniforms. Police! The dogs jumped up with a start, but they soon noticed that as well as human police officers, there were also three German Shepherd police dogs.

"Relax," the highest-ranking dog told them. "You're safe. And soon, you'll all be back in your own homes."

Petra's heart leapt. But the same couldn't be said for all of the dogs.

NINETEEN

The dogs were taken to a local police station where a vet came to give them a check-up and to find out their owners' details from the microchips. Humans soon started to turn up to claim their pets. The Daleys were the first to arrive.

Mr and Mrs Daley burst through the doors of the back room where the dogs were, with Lucy barging past them, desperate to see Petra. They rushed straight to her and swept her up into a massive hug.

"Petra puppy!" the Daleys squealed like excited children. "You're okay! You're coming home!" They sat down on some plastic chairs, and Petra climbed up onto Mr Daley's lap and into his arms.

"You big soft girl, Meister," Mr Daley chuckled, using one of his silly names. Have you missed your cuddles?"

"Oh, so that's what a cuddle is," said Baxter. He was pleased to see Petra reunited with her loving family but worried for himself and Buster. What would happen to them? The thieves had run away and wouldn't be coming forward to claim them. That was good, but where would they end up?

The Daleys stayed, wanting to ensure that all the dogs were reunited with their families before they took Petra home. The next to arrive was a young farmer who had tears in his eyes when Pepper jumped all over him, her tail wagging joyfully. After him came two hysterically happy women for Sprite, followed by a couple for Dusty with a huge white greyhound who were all overjoyed to see her. A family came for Storm. The two young humans cried with delight at seeing their best friend again and had to be prised off Storm by their parents when it was time to go.

Soon after they'd all gone, the vet, Wren Robbins, rushed in to pick up Gomez and Gizmo. After she'd dropped to the floor and covered both of their faces with kisses, she eventually remembered where she was. She stood to have a chat with the police officer.

"I expect the vet who's been earlier has told you that this dog has got an awful eye infection?" she said, pointing at Baxter. "And both of them have terribly overgrown toenails? I'm surprised they can walk at all."

Now Petra understood why the two big dogs were so slow on their journey. It wasn't just because they were unfit. They were also in pain with their long toenails. Neither of them had complained about it once. She remembered how evil she'd thought Baxter looked when she first saw him, with his volcano-rim red eyes. But it wasn't badness that made his eyes look that way. It was an untreated infection making them all sore. She made a note to add it to the other lessons she'd learned through this experience: don't be so quick to judge others.

"So, these dogs don't have a microchip, you say?" The vet was still talking to the police officer. "That's a bit suspicious. You think they belong to the thieves?"

"We do. We haven't managed to catch them yet, but I expect they've got a puppy farm going on somewhere. It's our guess that these lads were used to guard the place. They haven't been a bit of bother since they came here, but they look pretty intimidating, the size they are. I imagine they've got a big bark to go with it too. Don't know what we're going to do with them," the police officer replied.

"I can take them with me?" the vet offered. "I work with an animal rescue and rehoming charity called Peregrine Pets. I can give them the treatment they need and try and find them a home together."

"That sounds grand. Yes, you take them and find them some nice people to live with." The police officer grinned, loving a happy ending. "And what about this one?" She pointed at Bella, who was pressed up against Petra, now back on the floor with Lucy. "We've contacted her owners, and they've said they don't want her back. Said they made a mistake buying a puppy and asked us if we could rehome her. Could you take her to the rehoming place too?"

"They don't want her?" The vet was outraged. "Who wouldn't want a beautiful young Dalmatian like her? She's a bit grubby, but that'll soon wash off. She's perfect. Of course I'll take her. She'll get a new home that deserves her in no time."

"There's no need for that," said Mrs Daley looking at her husband, who smiled his agreement. "We'll take her. She can come and live with us if that's all right? We'd take the boys too if we could, but they're just too big for our house."

The police officer smiled so much the ends of her mouth nearly touched her ears. Something was done with paperwork, and then they were free to go. Gomez and Gizmo, Buster and Baxter left with the vet, after Gomez thanked Petra to the ends of the earth for making it possible, and Bella went with the Daleys to begin a new life. The young Dalmatian was the happiest she'd ever been, and she left the police station with a smile on her face to match the officer who was wiping away a tear of joy as she watched them go.

TWENTY

That night, after the dogs had a good meal and a bath, and Bella was presented with a temporary collar that Lucy grown had out of, it was time for bed.

"We'll have to go to the pet shop and get Bella a bed in the morning," said Mrs Daley. "I'll go in the attic and get some blankets for tonight."

"I don't think there's any need," said Mr Daley pointing at Petra's bed where Bella was snuggled in beside her, fast asleep. "It looks like she loves her Auntie Meist!" Mr Daley laughed at his new name for Petra.

When the Daleys turned off the light and went to bed, Lucy and Petra could finally speak to each other.

"Thank dog, you're home," said Lucy, sitting up in her bed. "I've been so worried about you! I thought you'd be back days ago. I was terrified that something had happened to you again. It was only yesterday when I saw you on the news that I knew you were okay."

"You didn't lose your spots again, did you?"

"No, but they did begin to fade. When you didn't come back, they started to go grey. That's why I thought something had gone wrong. But they didn't disappear like last time, so I still had hope. As soon as the phone rang and I heard someone telling the Daleys you'd been found, they went black again. I was so relieved."

Petra wasn't sure whether Lucy meant she was relieved that Petra was all right or that her spots had returned. As she was thinking about it, something else popped into her head.

"What do you mean, you saw me on the news?" she said, sitting upright too.

"It's a long story," said Lucy, launching into it. "When you went missing from the garden that day, the

Daleys went out looking for you straight away. They drove around all over, but they didn't find you, of course. They called the police, knocked on everyone's doors in the village and put up posters like last time. They offered a reward for your return. They'd heard about dogs being stolen in the area and were convinced someone had stolen you. They went on the computer and started doing something called 'social media'. They put pictures of you everywhere 'online'. They found other people whose dogs had gone missing, and they all joined together to spread the word.

Then, yesterday, something came on the news. A man who was walking home late at night saw a rowing boat on a lake. It seemed to be moving, but there was no-one in it. He filmed it on his phone as he thought he was imagining what he was seeing. He thought the boat was full of dogs but he knew it couldn't be. Until he watched it back. Then he saw that he was right – the boat was full of dogs, and something else. Two more dogs climbed out of the water. They'd been swimming behind the boat, pushing it along!

Well, obviously, he knew that was not normal. He sent it to a national news programme, and it was on the TV! Neighbourhood Watch groups in the area near the lake started running twenty-four-hour surveillance, looking out for the dogs. But it seems the thieves also saw the news. They put a drone up in the air – a flying camera – to search for you, and they found you. They came for you."

"They did. They would've got Buster and Baxter – all of us - but some help came at the last minute: the wasps." Petra told Lucy about how the wasps had come to their aid.

"That's how it was for me when I was desperate for help," Lucy said, remembering how she'd rescued Petra from the hole she'd fallen into earlier that year.

"Except it wasn't wasps who came to me. It was my own spots. Miracles *can* happen."

"But the thieves couldn't get away in their van. They had to run. Some people stopped them from driving away."

"Yes – the Neighbourhood Watch night shift person in that village had seen you pass through. They'd got in touch with people to go and get you, but the thieves had got there first. So the people did what they could to stop them getting away. Shame it didn't work."

A sudden thought popped into Petra's head and alarmed her so much, she leapt out of her bed. Doing so woke Bella up.

"What if the thieves don't get caught?" she said.

"I'm sure they will," Lucy assured her. "The people in the cars who tried to stop them took pictures of them on their phones. They'll be all over the news tomorrow.

They'll be seen. Those evil men won't be able to steal any more dogs."

"No, you don't understand," Petra said, pacing around the kitchen. "There were more dogs in the place where I found the ones I got out. Dogs with puppies who couldn't come with us. If the thieves don't go back there, there will be no-one to feed those dogs. No-one will know they're even there! What can we do?" She remembered her promise to the boxer. Petra had told her she'd go back for the others and help them too.

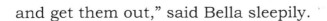

"We'll have to go and get them out," said Bella sleepily.

"But how?" asked Lucy. "How could we get there? Petra knows the way, but I bet she never gets let off the lead ever again now that she's gone missing twice. The Daleys won't let us out of their sight."

"That's just what I was thinking," agreed Petra. There was no way she'd be able to sneak off now.

"Don't worry," said Bella, mysteriously. "I know what we can do. I've got a plan."

THE END

Find out what Lucy, Petra and Bella get up to in

their next adventure in the sequel:

Jingle Bella
to the Rescue

Author's Note

Petra with Bella

Dogs have been a part of my life since I was six years old. My first dog was a cocker spaniel, and since then, I've always had a dog – or two! I couldn't be without them. They're the best friends anyone could wish for and are an important part of the family.

Because I love dogs, I'm always concerned when I hear stories of them being treated badly. Recently, I've been hearing about how more people have wanted to buy dogs and puppies, which has led to an increase in puppy farms and dog thefts. And that's where the idea for this story came from.

One of my favourite books as a child was the *Hundred and One Dalmatians*, where the puppies are famously stolen by Cruella De'Vil to be made into fur coats. This, of course, was made up, but dogs really do get stolen, and one of the main reasons for this is to use them in puppy farms.

Puppy farms are places where many dogs are kept in poor conditions and used repeatedly to produce litters of puppies. The owners of these farms are more concerned about making money than breeding happy, healthy puppies that will go to good homes. The welfare of the dogs is usually overlooked, and they are often kept in cramped, unclean conditions with no access to outdoor space for fresh air and exercise.

I hope that this story will help to highlight what dogs need from their owners and that owning a dog is a privilege and a responsibility. They give so much love, and bring so much joy, they deserve the very best care and attention we can give.

Getting a puppy? For more information on how to spot a puppy farm, visit

https://www.pdsa.org.uk/taking-care-of-your-pet/looking-after-your-pet/puppies-dogs/could-you-spot-a-puppy-farm

Thank You

I'm really proud of this story, but it hasn't been a one-woman effort. I've had plenty of help. Big thanks, first of all, to the pre-publication team who worked with me to get this book polished and perfected. Phoebe, Sarah, Kathryn, Evie, Tess, Daisy, Freddie, Ruby, Rohan, Martha, Angus, Jackson, Trenaii, and their mums, helped to proofread the manuscript, and offered their thoughts on title ideas and blurbs. Their support has been invaluable and I'm so grateful for their involvement.

I also worked with a number of schools to help me decide on the best title and blurb for the book so thank you to all the children and teachers for their votes and suggestions. It was wonderful to hear the thoughts behind their choices and I really enjoyed meeting some of them to talk about their responses through Zoom visits. Their feedback definitely helped me to make my mind up.

To Ruth Eastwood, my gratitude for answering all my questions related to greyhound racing.

Thanks again to the illustrator, Steve Hutton, for the fantastic cover and images in the book that really help to bring the story to life. Seeing the illustrations is one of my favourite parts of writing as I have the images in my head as the story is being created, but it's amazing when they become real and everyone else can see them too!

Amanda Horan at Let's Get Booked – as usual, her editing, formatting and advice is much appreciated and, as always, I've enjoyed working on this book with her.

Finally, to my mum for proofreading and my husband for listening to me talk about this story for months and in doing so, helping me get my ideas straight. Thank you!

About the Author

Helen lives in Cumbria with her husband and a family of horses, dogs, hens, ducks and geese! As well as writing books, she also teaches English and runs a secondary school library.

Visit **www.helenharaldsen.co.uk** to find out more about Helen and to sign up to her mailing list. You'll receive news, updates, opportunities and free, exclusive bonus material linked to HH Books.

Did you enjoy this book? The author would love to see your reviews on Amazon. Please feel free to post your comments and let others know about Petra and The Dogs in Danger.

Also By This Author

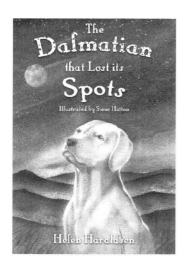

Did You Know?

Buster and Baxter are Tibetan Mastiffs. Mastiff-type dogs originated in Tibet around 5,000 years ago. They developed into two types: the Do-Khyi, who lived in villages or travelled with shepherds to guard their flock, and the larger Tsang-Khyi, which often served as guardians for the Tibetan Buddhist monks who lived there.

Little is known of the Tibetan Mastiff before 1800. In 1847, the first dog from Tibet was imported to England and given to Queen Victoria as a gift from the Viceroy of India.

Gizmo is a Staffordshire Bull Terrier. This breed was created in the early nineteenth century to be a small, fast fighting dog, yet gentle and friendly towards people.

Gomez is a pug. It is believed that the pug's name comes from the Latin word for "fist" because his face resembles a human fist. Pugs originated in China. Some historians believe they are related to the Tibetan Mastiff. They were prized by the Emperors of China and lived in luxury, sometimes even being guarded by soldiers.

In the early 1600s, pugs became favourites of royal households throughout Europe.

Pugs became very popular during the Victorian era. Queen Victoria had many pugs, and also bred them.

Dusty is a greyhound. The greyhound is an ancient breed that originated in the Middle East and North Africa. Greyhounds have been mentioned by Greeks, presented in art by Egyptians and are the only breed of dog mentioned in the Bible.

Greyhounds have been prized throughout history. Historic figures who loved this breed include Cleopatra and Queen Elizabeth I of England. The support of the two queens led to greyhound racing being dubbed the "Sport of Queens."

They found their way into Europe during the Dark Ages. They were so respected for their hunting skill that the laws of the time protected royal lands by forbidding anyone living within ten miles of the king's forests from owning a greyhound.

Storm is a husky. The Siberian Husky is believed to have originated among a tribe of Siberian nomads. They are among the oldest of dog breeds. The nomads used the dogs as transportation.

The Siberian Husky was imported to Alaska in 1908 and were used as sled dogs during the gold rush. Even today, they are used in the All-Alaska Sweepstakes, which is a 408-mile dogsled race.

Pepper is a border collie. The breed has been around since humans in Britain first began using dogs to help guard and herd sheep. In the border country between Scotland and England, the herding dog became one of the most valuable assets a shepherd could have.

In 1876 R.J. Lloyd Price began sheepdog trials. He brought 100 wild Welsh sheep to the Alexandra Palace in London for a demonstration. The spectators were astonished by the dogs, whose only assistance from their handlers was in the form of hand signals and whistles.

Today the border collie is recognised as the premier sheepherding dog.

Sprite is a short-haired dachshund. These dogs were created in Germany, where they were known as the badger dog, 'dachs' meaning badger and 'hund' meaning dog. As well as badgers, dachshunds were also used for hunting other den animals such as foxes and rabbits.

The breed was developed over the course of many years in the 18th and 19th centuries. The purpose was to develop a fearless, elongated dog that could dig into burrows.

Today the dachshund is the only breed that hunts both above and below ground. Their short, powerful legs enable dachshunds to go deep into narrow tunnels to pursue their prey. Their unusually large and paddle-shaped paws are perfect for efficient digging.

Bella, like Lucy, is a Dalmatian. The breed can be traced back to the region of Dalmatia in Croatia. They were often used in the 18th and 19th century as companions for the carriages of the wealthy to protect the occupants from highwaymen. Dalmatians also played a vital role with the fire service, back in the days when steam-powered pumpers were pulled by horses. Dalmatians would run alongside the horses helping to clear the way in crowded streets.

Petra – The Poltermeist – is a German Shorthaired Pointer. These dogs were bred in Germany as a hunting dog that could effectively hunt all types of game on all types of land, from dense forests to open fields. The dog's job was to locate the game and point – remain still – to allow the hunters time to close in on the prey. It was also needed to retrieve fallen game both on land and in water.

Finally, if you've been wondering why some dogs have capital letters for their breed names and some don't, I'll explain. Most dog breed names are common nouns so do not need capital letters (e.g. poodle). But where a proper noun is used as part of the name, such as a place name, that does need a capital letter (e.g. German Shepherd).

Printed in Great Britain
by Amazon